RAILROAD TO REDEMPTION

The influx of railroad men looking to build a new track to Redemption brings trouble for Sheriff Cassidy Yates. But when Dayton Fisher arrives, looking for work, things seem to be looking up. And his bravery persuades Luther to hire him as a bodyguard. However, when he also takes on gunslingers to cause mayhem about town, Luther is killed and suddenly Dayton is pitted against his friend Cassidy. Can the two men be reconciled and defeat the gunslingers?

I. J. PARNHAM

◆

RAILROAD
TO
REDEMPTION

Complete and Unabridged

LINFORD
Leicester

First published in Great Britain in 2010 by
Robert Hale Limited
London

First Linford Edition
published 2011
by arrangement with
Robert Hale Limited
London

British Library CIP Data

Parnham, I. J.
  Railroad to redemption. - -
  (Linford western library)
  1. Western stories.
  2. Large type books.
  I. Title II. Series
  823.9′2–dc22

  ISBN 978–1–4448–0916–9

Published by
F. A. Thorpe (Publishing)
Anstey, Leicestershire

Set by Words & Graphics Ltd.
Anstey, Leicestershire
Printed and bound in Great Britain by
T. J. International Ltd., Padstow, Cornwall

This book is printed on acid-free paper

1

The commotion was growing.

People were clamouring to get closer to the station house while others were barging people aside in their eagerness to get away. Already several passengers were lying on the platform and curling up as they tried to avoid getting trampled.

From fifty yards away Dayton Fisher couldn't tell what was causing the consternation, but he welcomed the distraction. It meant he could slip away into town unseen.

He rolled his legs down from the doorway of the freight car, took one last look along the length of the train to ensure nobody was looking his way, then jumped down on to the platform.

He batted the straw and dirt from his clothes to appear presentable, then walked off towards the station house. On the way he considered the trouble, as everyone else was, while trying to look as if he'd disembarked in the same way as the other passengers had.

In reality he'd spent the last two days cooped up in the car behind two large crates. His only sustenance had been the water bottle he'd filled before he'd hidden himself away and the hunk of bread he'd bought with his last few cents.

He'd had no destination in mind. He'd just stayed hidden until he couldn't cope with the hunger and the cold wind whistling through the car any longer.

Then again, he figured, the town of Monotony was very much like any other and no matter where he got off he had to find employment. And he had to find it quickly while he still had the strength to do a day's work.

Closer to the station house he heard the first explanation of what was happening.

'It's a raid,' someone shouted. 'He's taken a hostage.'

This revelation made the men who had been peering through the door back away, but with so many others crowding behind them, this movement only added to the commotion.

The first hint of order came when a tall man with a star arrived. With a few brisk commands he ordered the people before him to move out of his way and let him get closer to the trouble.

The people were slow to move aside and so the lawman had yet to reach the door when Dayton decided he wasn't that interested in seeing how this incident played out. He faced the town's main drag then ran his gaze along the many establishments, wondering where he should ask about work first.

A gunshot tore out, creating sudden quiet.

Within moments everyone decided that they too weren't that interested in watching the incident. They scampered away with only the lawman advancing, but before he reached the station house a man charged through the door, a gun brandished. He took in the scene of the dozens of people surrounding him then roved the gun in a steady arc across the gathering.

'Get out of my way,' he demanded.

Nobody wasted time in raising their hands and moving back. Then, with a neat sideways movement, he sidled along beside the station house, choosing the direction where only one man was in his way: Dayton Fisher.

Dayton did as the others had done and backed away for a pace and raised his hands. The man gave him only the briefest of glances to confirm he wouldn't give him any trouble, but then he had a bigger problem to contend with.

'Stop!' a strident voice said from behind him. 'This is Sheriff Cassidy Yates.'

The man looked over his shoulder to see that space had now cleared around the lawman. Without warning, the man blasted off a wild shot that kicked shards from the station wall before it cannoned away.

Then the man rounded the corner, but the moment he disappeared from the lawman's view, he dropped to one knee and turned. From his new unexpected position he slipped back around the corner and tore off a volley of quick shots. Again the shots were wild, but they were worrying enough to make most people dive to the timbers while in self-preservation the lawman scrambled into hiding in the station house.

The man nodded to himself, as if he'd got the reaction he'd wanted. Then he jumped to his feet and hurried off into town.

Dayton was the only person on his side of the station and so he was the only one to see the shooter's hurried departure down the main drag and towards an alley beside the nearest saloon. So, when the lawman emerged from the station house, he called out to him, but Cassidy didn't look his way as he already had another problem to deal with.

'There's another raider!' someone shouted, pointing at another man fleeing in the opposite direction to the first man. 'And that one stole from me.'

This fleeing man had a slighter build than the previous man had, but he did have one advantage. He'd left a horse beside the station and, with an athletic leap, ran for a discarded crate, bounced off it, and vaulted on to the horse.

Before anyone could give chase, the man was galloping away heading out of town.

While Cassidy made up his mind which person to chase, Dayton glanced into town. The shooter had disappeared from view, and so he gestured over his head to get the lawman's attention.

'You get the rider,' he called out. 'I saw where the other one went.'

Cassidy considered him. Dayton doubted he'd be impressed by what he saw. Two days spent crumpled up in the freight car had done nothing to improve his appearance, which had been bedraggled before he'd got on the train. But Cassidy must have seen something that gave him confidence as he gave a brief nod then turned away.

Dayton then hurried off into town. He ran at a steady pace, still feeling unsure as to why he was giving chase. He was unarmed and his quarry was both armed and willing to shoot.

When he was closer to the saloon he looked over his shoulder and was pleased to see that several men were following him from the station. Dayton waited for them to catch up with him.

'He went that way,' he shouted, pointing down the side of the saloon.

The line of determined and grim-faced men hurried past him. To each man Dayton repeated his explanation of what he'd seen then slapped him on the back.

He also noted that most of the pursuers were armed and so when the last man had run past him, he took stock of the situation. The thought came that fleeing down the alley was an odd thing for the man to have done. The saloon and surrounding buildings marked the edge of town with the bulk of the town being in the other direction.

Unless the man had also left a horse there to effect an escape, he would probably double back into town. With everybody having run behind the saloon, Dayton decided to stay on the main drag, and so he set off at a brisk pace.

As he sprinted along he looked ahead for someone slipping around a building, but saw nobody and instead gathered a few bemused glances of his own from people who didn't know about the incident at the station.

From the other side of the buildings cries went up, proving that the pursuit was still under way. Feeling heartened, he speeded up and so was running as fast as he could when he ran around the final building and was confronted by the sight of his quarry coming in the other direction.

The man was looking over his shoulder and so at first he didn't register that Dayton was in his way. Then he tried to side-step around him, but their shoulders collided.

The force knocked Dayton into the wall while his quarry went to one knee. The man put out a hand to steady himself then jerked his other hand up, aiming his brandished gun at him.

With only a moment to react Dayton kicked out. The toe of his boot connected with the gun and sent it flying. Then he leapt at the man, slamming him on to his back.

All the air blasted from the man's chest as Dayton landed on him. Then he grabbed his arms and pinned him down, bearing down with all his weight.

They locked gazes. Then the man rolled his shoulders and with a grunt of effort, bucked Dayton away. The several days he'd gone with only a small amount of sustenance had weakened Dayton more than he had thought and so the shove sent him rolling away.

Shouting went up behind him as the pursuers closed. His assailant got to his knees and looked at them and then at his gun. He made an instant decision to ignore the weapon and moved to get to his feet, but while lying on his side Dayton thrust out a hand and grabbed his ankle.

The man kicked backwards, trying to tear his leg away, but Dayton held on and even managed to wrap a second hand around his leg. Dayton was dragged along for several paces, but, cheered by the cries and footfalls of the approaching chasers, he clung on.

Then in a blur of motion two men reached him and bundled the man to the ground. Other pursuers surrounded him with guns drawn and aimed at their captured quarry.

As the captured man was dragged to his feet, a supportive hand slapped down on Dayton's shoulder and a friendly face smiled at him.

'Let go now, stranger,' the man said. 'We've got him.'

Dayton breathed a sigh of relief and got to his feet where he received a round of enthusiastic backslaps.

Presently a red-faced and flustered man wearing a deputy sheriff's star arrived, then smiled on seeing that the situation was under control.

'You caught him,' he declared, setting his hands on his hips.

'We did the easy part, Deputy Judson,' one man said, pointing at Dayton. 'This man caught him.'

With everyone looking at him, Dayton introduced himself.

'I'm Dayton Fisher,' he said. 'I just arrived on the train.'

This comment generated another round of hearty back-slapping.

'Then, Dayton Fisher,' the deputy said, shaking his hand. 'Welcome to Monotony.'

* * *

Sheriff Cassidy Yates was closing in on his quarry.

The five-mile pursuit out of town had only irritated him even more than he had already been, as he didn't know what the other raider at the station was now doing.

He hoped that nobody had been hurt in the attempt to catch the armed man because his quarry didn't appear to be armed. Instead he was concentrating on his riding, but after five miles his horse was tiring. Ahead were three wagons that had been drawn up to form a loose semicircle and the rider was heading towards them.

Cassidy gathered a burst of speed from his mount aiming to catch him before he reached the wagons so as to avoid dragging innocent people into the final showdown. But the rider must have had the same thought as he spurred his horse on.

Amongst the wagons people were milling around and watching the approaching riders with interest. Cassidy waved and shouted at them to stay back, but none of them moved.

Cassidy didn't gain on the rider and, twenty yards from the wagons, his quarry leapt down from his horse with the same agility as he'd used to get on it, then carried on running. Cassidy stayed on his horse and continued the chase as the man headed for a gap between two wagons.

Someone shouted at them. Cassidy couldn't hear the words, but the intervention made the man look back then flinch on seeing how close behind him Cassidy was. This movement let Cassidy see he was young and fresh-faced.

Cassidy was looming over him when the man ran through the gap, but the moment Cassidy emerged on the other side he swung his legs round and jumped down from his horse.

He landed on his target's back, his momentum poleaxing him. With his captive splayed out beneath him, Cassidy gathered his breath. Then he rocked back on his heels and drew his gun.

'Make another wrong move,' he said, 'and it'll be your last.'

All he got by way of a response was a pained and high-pitched bleat, but Cassidy took no chances and, as he stood, he kept his gun trained on his captive. From the corner of his eye he saw that people were gathering. He gestured at them to keep back.

'I'm Sheriff Cassidy Yates,' he said. 'And this man is my prisoner.'

'And what,' a woman said from beside him, 'do you want with her?'

'Her?' Cassidy murmured.

He turned to the speaker, then did a double-take. The woman was a nun, and for that matter so were all the people closing in on him.

'Yes. That was a most unseemly way for you to treat Sister Cynthia. What do you have to say to excuse yourself?'

Cassidy looked down again at his captive and this time he appraised the slim build and the foreshortened view of neck and face in a different light.

His captive was a woman, a young

one, and possibly a nun too.

'I'm sorry,' he offered.

★   ★   ★

The first bullet kicked splinters from the door frame; the second slug tore through the open doorway and cannoned into the far wall.

Then they came.

One man took up a position beside the door outside while the other man charged inside. The two Bell brothers, Jackson and Eddie, were waiting for him.

Their assailants had recklessly assumed that the days of continual attacks had pushed them to breaking point, but the brothers were fighting for their lives and they were as determined as they had ever been.

So the man who ran in didn't even manage to pick out where the two brothers were hiding in the darkened recesses of the house before twin shots tore into his chest. He ran on for several stumbling paces before folding then keeling over and ploughing into the far wall where he collapsed into a crumpled heap.

The other man jerked into the doorway and, using the sound of gunfire, picked out Eddie with unerring accuracy. He raised his rifle, but before he could fire, Jackson caught him with a low shot to the belly that sent him spinning into the wall, his own shot wasting itself in the roof.

Eddie's deadly shot to the heart dispatched him for good.

Then the two brothers waited with bated breath to see if that had been the prelude for a more sustained assault, but long moments passed in silence.

Jackson unfolded his legs and got to his feet. He took a cautious route to the first body and, with Eddie covering him, he turned the body over.

A grunt of contentment was his only comment.

Only when he'd checked on the second body did the brothers allow themselves to relax.

'You fine?' Jackson asked.

'Yeah,' Eddie said. 'You reckon that's the last of 'em?'

'I guess we'll find out soon enough.'

With that comment Jackson slipped over to the door and risked a glance outside to survey the terrain. Then he jerked back and slammed his back to the wall. Even before he spoke Eddie knew the answer to his question.

'More of them out there?' he asked.

'Sure,' Jackson said.

2

'Sorry isn't good enough,' said the nun who had identified herself as Sister Angelica.

'I didn't know he was a she,' Cassidy Yates said, then shrugged. 'If you know what I mean.'

'If that is your only excuse for your unruly behaviour,' Sister Angelica said, walking past Cassidy towards the still prone woman, 'then it would have been better if you'd have kept your mouth shut.'

Sister Angelica knelt down beside Cynthia and helped her to a sitting position. For her part Cynthia looked up at Cassidy with an aggrieved glare while rubbing her back where Cassidy had landed so heavily. Sister Angelica had to help her to her feet.

'I can't do that,' Cassidy said, although he did holster his gun. 'This woman stole while she was in Monotony.'

'She did not. She is a novice nun of the Sisters of the Sacred Cross. To even suggest she would lower herself to such an activity is an insult to us all.'

Cassidy said nothing and instead looked at the young woman who was shamefaced and refusing to meet his eye. She wasn't wearing a habit as the others were, at least excusing his mistake, even if Sister Angelica didn't see it that way.

Cynthia rocked from foot to foot, gulped several times, then finally risked looking at Sister Angelica.

'But I did,' she said finally.

The nun rounded on her. 'You couldn't have.'

'I'm sorry, Sister Angelica. I cannot lie.' She turned to Cassidy. 'I went into town to see if we could reach Bleak Point by train. We couldn't, but I got caught up in some trouble. Then this man dropped some bills. I picked them up. I shouldn't have, but we have little money and. . . . '

She took an uncertain pace towards him and extracted a folded wad from her pocket. Cassidy took the offered money and unfolded the bills to find she had taken three dollars.

Sister Angelica noted how much money was involved then folded her arms and favoured Cassidy with another harsh glare.

'She may have been in error in appropriating discarded money, but was holding on to such a trifling sum worth you pursuing her here and then accosting her?'

'It was. It's my duty.' Cassidy tucked the money into a pocket. 'So can you vouch that she's with you and that she wasn't in league with the man who was shooting up the station?'

'I most certainly can vouch that she is with us and she most certainly would not have had anything to do with a man, whether he be shooting up a station or not.'

'Then I won't pursue the matter and I'll entrust you with disciplining her as you deem fit.'

Sister Angelica considered this statement, presumably looking for something to pick fault with, then conceded Cassidy's offer with a short bow.

Cassidy tipped his hat to her, Cynthia and the three other nuns. Then he turned to go, but Sister Angelica raised a hand, bidding him to stay.

'As you have concluded that minor matter,' she declared, 'you can make amends for your mistake by aiding us with a more important concern: how do we get to Bleak Point?'

Cassidy shook his head. 'You don't. It's a dangerous journey and Bleak Point isn't a fit place for womenfolk, even thieving ones like Cynthia.'

Sister Angelica bristled at Cassidy's sarcasm. 'I didn't ask for judgement on our actions, just advice on how we can reach our destination.'

'Then if you won't listen to sense, you'll need a heap of luck to find a guide who'll risk his life going there with a bunch of nuns. How long you survive once you get there depends on how many guns you have.'

Sister Angelica reached into her habit and held out the cross she wore around her neck.

'The Sisters of the Sacred Cross have all the protection we need, but for your information we did have a guide who escorted us from Beaver Ridge. He abandoned us at Carmon.'

Cassidy felt a surge of sympathy for this man, but he limited himself to a smile before he moved towards his horse.

'Then I wish you luck in finding his replacement.'

'We don't need luck; we need you to find us someone who'll take us there.'

Cassidy stomped to a halt and turned.

'So you want me, a lawman, to delay finding the man who was shooting up the station so that I can find you a guide?' Cassidy set his hands on his hips.

Sister Angelica smiled for the first time. 'I'm pleased you have finally understood your duties. Now stop standing around wasting our time and escort us to Monotony.'

★ ★ ★

'If I can help with anything else,' Dayton Fisher said, 'let me know.'

'We'll be sure to do that,' Deputy Evan Judson said with a glance at the door to the sheriff's office.

Obligingly the other deputy sheriff, Floyd Wright, opened the door.

Although Evan's tone and demeanour were encouraging him to leave, Dayton dallied before the deputy's desk as he wondered how he could turn the conversation back to the subject of his actions.

When he'd chased after the fleeing man, he hadn't done so in the hope of getting a reward. But now that the excitement of the chase was over, he couldn't help but think that even a few coins would get him a meal and a bath and give him a better chance of finding work.

He was preparing to swallow his

pride and ask if the deputies had any spare change when the door opened and Sheriff Cassidy Yates returned.

'The raider?' Cassidy asked.

'Behind bars,' Floyd said, gesturing to the cells at the back of the office.

Cassidy looked to the cells to consider the new prisoner. He smiled.

'You two did better than I did.'

Floyd nodded, clearly having noted that Cassidy had returned without a prisoner and deciding it was best not to question him about what had happened.

'We didn't do well.' Floyd gestured to Evan then Dayton. 'Evan made the arrest, but the hard work was down to Dayton Fisher here.'

Cassidy turned to Dayton. 'You caught him?'

Dayton shrugged, now finding that given a chance to speak he didn't feel like overstating his actions.

'I had plenty of help,' he said. 'Just about the whole town joined in to drag him here.'

'He's being too modest,' Evan said.

'Everyone says our prisoner would have got away if it hadn't been for Dayton. And he was unarmed, but that didn't stop him tackling the raider.'

'Then you're a welcome visitor to town,' Cassidy said. He glanced outside at the three wagons that had just stopped outside the hotel. 'Unlike others.'

'I hope the rest of the townsfolk are as hospitable.' Dayton took a deep breath. 'I'm looking for work.'

Cassidy considered this information, nodding.

'In that case I'll ask around until I find someone who'll help you.'

'Obliged,' Dayton said.

Cassidy turned to Evan. 'What was the prisoner doing at the station?'

'He won't talk, but as far as I can piece together it wasn't a raid. He rode into town then waited for this business-man who had arrived on the train. He dragged him into the station house, but what he planned to do with him then, I don't know yet.'

'Who was the businessman?'

'I was,' a voice said from behind him. 'Luther Chisholm.'

Dayton glanced past Cassidy to see that a smartly dressed man was standing in the doorway.

'Do you know the man who attacked you?' Cassidy asked.

Luther came into the law office. 'No.'

'Or what he wanted?'

Luther spread his hands. 'I have many business interests, so I have many enemies.'

Cassidy considered this cryptic answer, then gestured to Dayton.

'Then it was good for you that you have one friend in town. Dayton stepped in and caught your attacker.'

Luther appraised Dayton, then delivered a short bow.

'I am in your debt, sir. My attacker was armed and trigger-happy and yet you, an unarmed man, caught him.'

Dayton nodded while he debated whether to press home his advantage or underplay it.

'I did what I could,' he said finally.

'But you did more than most.' Luther rubbed his chin. 'And so as I will be in town for a while and you are without gainful employment, I'd like to offer you a job.'

Dayton acknowledged Luther's shrewd assessment of his status with a wide smile.

'I'll take it.' He thought for a moment. 'Doing what?'

Luther smiled at the order of Dayton's responses.

'You have already helped me once by catching my attacker; I'd like you to continue to keep me safe.'

★　★　★

'You ready to talk yet?'

The prisoner glared at Cassidy from his cot, his jaw set firm with an exaggerated show of being quiet.

'You'll have to speak soon,' Cassidy continued, 'because if you don't, I'll conclude the worst possible motives for what you did, which includes the attempted murder of the several dozen people who were at the station.'

The prisoner's calm expression wavered as Cassidy's bluff had the desired effect. In reality, after having questioned the bystanders, it was clear he had resorted to gunfire only to aid his escape when he'd been cornered by an intrigued crowd. So the prisoner would have little to worry about, but he wouldn't know that.

'And then there's the matter of you shooting at a lawman and your attempted train robbery. After committing those crimes, you'll be lucky to ever stand on the other side of those bars.'

'You can't pin all that on me,' the prisoner snapped.

'So you can talk, after all.' Cassidy smiled as he moved closer to the bars. 'So why not tell me your side of the story and stop me having to work out my own version?'

The prisoner muttered to himself, acknowledging that Cassidy had won that battle of wits. Then he smirked, as if a new battle was about to begin.

'I won't talk. But if you want to clear this up, tell Luther Chisholm who I am. He won't want charges pressed against me.'

'And who are you?'

'Nelson Mann.'

Then he locked his hands behind his head and made a show of resting comfortably on his cot while he awaited his release.

3

'They must be waiting until it's dark,' Eddie Bell said, more to ease his own nerves than because he thought Jackson hadn't realized this.

Jackson turned away from looking out of the window to nod, his face set dourly.

The earlier euphoria of having defeated the two gunslingers who had stormed into their house had now receded and had been replaced with the usual tired fortitude.

They had remained inside for the last three days, refusing to relent to the men outside no matter when they came. Each man had slept fitfully while the other had stayed on guard, going about their duty with grim efficiency. The disagreement with their youngest brother Sherman about their tactics had been the only sour note.

Accordingly, and not for the first time, Jackson mentioned the subject, probably to take his mind off the next battle.

'Do you reckon there's any chance that Sherman got help?' he asked.

'Nobody in Redemption cares about us.' Eddie took a deep breath. 'But we saw what happened. He's dead.'

Jackson frowned. 'He probably is, but that doesn't stop me hoping we got it wrong.'

Eddie nodded and, like Jackson, he looked at the gorge that opened up before their house and then up to the top of the ridge to their right, the last place they'd seen their youngest brother alive.

Their house nestled at the entrance to Redemption Gorge where the rocky sides towered above them. A river meandered by and the land was fertile, this rare oasis having originally attracted them to settle there. Recesses on either side of the gorge created an X shape and so they had called their home the Bar X, somewhat optimistically, in the hope of a better life to come when they would run their own ranch.

Beyond the X the land rose towards the Barren Plains and then to the silver mine eighty miles on at Bleak Point. Behind them was the town of Redemption some ten miles away.

Three days ago railroad men had arrived with threats and ultimatums, but they'd been met with arguments and hot lead. A stand-off had developed until, at sundown, Sherman had tired of the siege and had gone off to get help.

His brothers didn't reckon he would get any, but he had been adamant. He knew the terrain and so he had taken what he had hoped would be the least expected route away. He had crossed the base of the gorge and climbed the ridge in the recess to their right without trouble. But when he'd reached the top, someone had been waiting for him.

Too far away to help, Eddie and Jackson could only screw up their eyes and watch what happened next. To their horror they'd seen Sherman's form, silhouetted against the twilit sky beyond, fold over then tumble from view on the other side of the ridge. The crack of a gunshot had reached them a few moments later.

Until that moment the stand-off had been bloodless, but the shooting changed everything and set them on a confrontation they could never turn away from. Now most of the railroad men responsible had paid with their lives, but that image still haunted Eddie's thoughts.

With a grunt to himself he tore his gaze away from the ridge, knowing that looking up there in the hope that Sherman would come striding back into view was hopeless. Instead, he looked to the entrance to the gorge.

Their assailants had hidden themselves behind a tumble of boulders at the entrance a hundred yards away. Rills and rocks provided cover on the way to the house, but not all the way. So Eddie wasn't surprised when he saw movement fifty yards away as a man scurried from one boulder to the next.

A few moments later a second man followed the previous man's route. Eddie and Jackson stayed their fire, knowing the final twenty yards over open ground was the most dangerous.

'Just the two?' Eddie asked.

'It looks like it,' Jackson said, turning to smile at Eddie with the first hopeful look he'd provided in days.

They were unsure how many men had come originally, but as the days had passed they had counted the remaining ambushers, and two was how many they had hoped were left.

'Then maybe we won't need to wait for Sherman to bring help.'

Jackson grunted his support for this optimistic outlook. Then they waited. Darkness was descending, making the boulder behind which the men were hiding harder to discern.

The full moon they'd enjoyed over the last few days had ensured that night attacks had lost most of their effectiveness. But now the moon wouldn't rise until several hours after sundown, which meant they would come early.

The light level continued to drop until the ridge ahead had become merely a dark absence of stars; then Eddie first caught movement ahead. He narrowed his eyes trying to discern exactly where it was. He heard Jackson shuffle to the side by his own window as he too clearly saw something, although neither man spoke.

Then a flash of light exploded from the ground as a slug whined and ripped Eddie's hat from his head. Eddie didn't waste time pondering on his luck and returned fire at the point of light.

Jackson joined him and slugs clattered off stones, but they all failed to find a target. The shooter had fired then moved.

Pounding footfalls heralded his next actions as the man moved for the blind spot at the side of the small house.

Eddie fired into the darkness, spraying his gunfire in a long arc. He was rewarded with a cry of pain and a thud as the man failed to reach his destination. Jackson also fired at the spot, this time repeatedly, so presumably he could see where the man had fallen and was able to dispose of him.

That left just the one man.

They didn't have to wait long to find out what he'd do next as a hand jerked in through Jackson's window and splayed gunfire around. Clearly both assailants had made a run to the opposite sides of the house.

Jackson threw himself to the ground to avoid the wild gunfire that kicked and cannoned around the small room.

Eddie didn't wait for a stray slug to catch him and he rolled forward through the window. The low-built house meant he was close to the ground, so he fell the three feet to land on his side then rolled twice.

Then, with his hands thrust out straight, he picked out the man standing beside the other window. The man was jerking round to follow his progress but he'd already fired his six-shooter six times and was trying to back away around the corner.

Eddie caught him with a high shot to the shoulder that sent him spinning into the wall. A low shot to the back pinned him there; he stood upright for a moment, then slid bonelessly to the ground.

Eddie lay poised, listening, but all was silent until Jackson slipped out of the house to examine the dead man and then the earlier man they'd dispatched.

Then he came over and held out a hand to drag Eddie to his feet.

'I doubted it a few times,' he said. 'But we survived.'

'Wrong,' Eddie said, unwilling to let their good fortune cheer him. 'Only two of us did.'

★ ★ ★

'Are you enjoying your new job?' Sheriff Cassidy Yates asked.

Dayton Fisher smiled. Despite his desperate need for work, when Luther had offered him the job he had been minded to refuse, as he didn't want to be, effectively, a hired gun.

Now, with Luther having paid to have him outfitted in new clothes, with his belly full and a hotel room to himself, he was glad he'd put aside his misgivings.

Best of all, after his disastrous first few minutes in town, Luther's concerns about him facing trouble hadn't materialized.

'So far it's been ideal,' Dayton said. He raised his whiskey glass and winked.

Cassidy smiled, acknowledging his meaning that any job that involved spending the night in the Golden Star couldn't be faulted.

'Where's Luther?'

Dayton pointed to the stairs. 'He's in his room. He'll come down soon and apparently he'll pay for any drinks I order while I wait.'

Dayton downed his whiskey then poured another drink and one for Cassidy.

The lawman took the drink. 'Then you got yourself the ideal job and it's no less than you deserve.'

Dayton accepted that assessment with a sigh. He gnawed his lip as he pondered, then decided that with a fresh start beckoning he didn't want to face any problems later.

'Some might say it's better than I deserve.' He swirled his drink then leaned on the bar to look down into his glass. 'I was living in Bear Creek, but I had some trouble and I had to leave.'

Cassidy adopted Dayton's posture. 'Are you sure you should be telling a lawman this?'

'I reckon so, because there's nothing to tell, but if I don't say anything and you hear about it later, it could sound worse than it was.'

'I understand. Go on.'

'I was working in a mercantile, but the owner wasn't making any money. One day he accused me of stealing. I hadn't, but I knew who had and that was his good-for-nothing son. I couldn't tell him that and so it looked bad for me. I got run out of town.'

Cassidy considered this story while looking at Dayton, then downed his whiskey.

'You know something, Dayton? I believe you. If that problem follows you here, I'll help.'

'Then I'm glad I mentioned it.'

With that subject concluded, both men stood in companionable silence for a while until Dayton pointed out that Luther was coming down the stairs. Cassidy leaned towards him.

'Has he told you why he's in town yet?'

'Nope, and I reckon he doesn't want to talk about it.'

'I know. When I told him the prisoner's name was Nelson Mann, he didn't want to pursue the matter. That meant Nelson's crime amounted to him firing a gun.' Cassidy provided a rueful smile. 'If I charged everyone who did that, the whole town would be behind bars. So I had to let Nelson go.'

'Then I need to keep on the lookout for him.' Dayton pushed his unfinished drink away. 'But if I learn anything, I'll let you know.'

Cassidy acknowledged his offer of help with a curt nod. Then together they moved from the bar to welcome Luther. They exchanged pleasantries before heading to the door together.

'Business going well?' Cassidy said when they pushed through the batwings.

'It is,' Luther said, his slight smile acknowledging that he was being guarded in his response.

'Any sign of trouble erupting again?'

'No, but then again that's why I employed Dayton.'

Cassidy opened his mouth to continue pressing, but then stomped to a halt. A nun was blocking his way.

'Sheriff Cassidy Yates,' she proclaimed, waggling a reproachful finger at him, 'instead of finding us a guide, you are frittering away your time indulging in the evils of liquor.'

'You're wrong,' Cassidy said with a

sigh. 'Instead of finding you a guide I was doing my job.'

As the nun muttered to herself, Luther tipped his hat to them and then, with Dayton at his side, they continued down the road.

Dayton looked back to see that the nun was haranguing Cassidy while gesticulating angrily at the saloon. With his conversation with Cassidy tapping at his mind, Dayton decided to tentatively broach the subject that had concerned the lawman.

'Now that you're going about your business, you need to tell me what kind of dangers you might face.'

'There may be none. You just need to be vigilant in case Nelson acts again.'

'And anyone else?'

Luther stopped and gave Dayton a warning frown.

'I employed you because you looked as if you were the kind of man who didn't ask too many questions.'

'I am,' Dayton said, judging that he couldn't say anything else, although he reckoned Luther really meant he looked like a man who was so desperate for work he wouldn't ask too many questions. 'I just wanted to know what kind of business you're in.'

'Railroads,' Luther said before moving on with a determined stride that said that was all the explanation Dayton would get.

So Dayton remained silent as they headed down the road. To his surprise he found that their destination was the darkened station house.

The ticket office was closed but the waiting room door was open, even if the room itself was in darkness. Inside, two men were loitering in the shadows.

'Luther Chisholm?' one man asked when they entered.

'I am. Where are the rest?'

'We came on ahead to check things were what they seemed. If they are, we'll meet again tomorrow.'

Luther nodded then gestured for Dayton to shut the door behind them.

When Dayton had done as requested,

his eyes accustomed to the gloom only slowly, so the men remained shrouded in shadows. Only their eyes picked up stray beams of light and conveyed their surly confidence.

'Is he all you have?' the second man asked.

'When I'm amongst friends, he is all I need.'

Luther spread his hands, then waited until both men conceded this point with a non-committed grunt. Then he moved a hand to a pocket.

The action made both men narrow their eyes so he slowed the motion and let just two fingers disappear from view. When they reappeared, a folded wad of bills was clutched between them.

'That won't be enough,' one man said.

'You're not enough,' Luther said, holding out the money. 'But this is the first payment so that we can have that meeting tomorrow.'

The man took the bills and unfolded them. He nodded, then looked up.

'Then maybe we can talk.'

44

'I need to warn you,' Dayton said, 'that a whole heap of trouble could be heading your way.'

Cassidy sighed then drew Dayton down to the quieter end of the bar.

'What's wrong?'

'I'm now sure that Luther's business dealings are illegal. Earlier tonight he set up a deal with some dangerous sounding men.'

Cassidy nodded. 'What deal?'

'I don't know. They were in the dark and they didn't give names, but it's got something to do with the railroad, and they're meeting up again at sundown tomorrow on the bridge at Spinner's Gulch.'

Cassidy leaned on the bar beside him, considering this information.

'Plenty of railroad men have been in town recently. There's a rumour they're planning to build a track up to the mine at Bleak Point. Perhaps it's to do with that.'

'So you're saying I have nothing to worry about and this is legitimate business?'

Cassidy snorted a laugh. 'I didn't say that. Railroad men may conduct legitimate business deals, but some of the men they hire to carry them out aren't.'

Dayton sighed. 'Then I need some advice, Cassidy. Do I keep on working for Luther, or do I turn my back on him?'

'Bearing in mind how desperate you are for work, it does you credit that you're prepared to walk away from him, but I'd prefer it if you went to that meeting.' Cassidy patted him on the back. 'Because I'll be there too making sure I get some answers.'

4

'How much longer do we have to wait?' Dayton asked, even though the sun had barely disappeared from view behind him.

'Patience,' Luther said. 'They said they'll come at sundown and these people always keep their word.'

Dayton leaned forward in the saddle to consider the railroad bridge ahead.

'I'd find it easier to be patient if I knew what this meeting was about and how many men are coming.'

'You have nothing to worry about. These men aren't the people I hired you to keep away.'

Dayton was wondering whether he should push his luck by pressing for more details when Luther raised a hand and pointed. Coming onto the bridge from the opposite direction was a line of riders, picking their way with steady care.

Luther glanced at Dayton to check he'd seen them. Then he jumped down from his horse and removed the saddle-bag, which he looped over a shoulder.

He and Dayton set off on foot onto the bridge. Dayton looked along the sides of Spinner's Gulch, concerned that Nelson Mann might have positioned himself somewhere where he could take a shot at Luther.

The sides of the gulch were precipitous with a 200-foot drop to the winding river below, which, with the low level of rainfall recently, was boulder strewn and signalled instant death to anyone who fell from the bridge.

On both sides of the gulch were caves and ledges upon which sparse pines grew. Dayton judged they could easily provide cover for a hidden assailant and with the light dropping that cover would be getting more effective all the while.

'This is far enough,' Dayton said. He

pointed to their side of the gulch. 'If there's any trouble, we can get back to our side quickly.'

Luther accepted this request without comment and so thirty yards out on to the bridge they stopped and waited.

Twenty yards from them the six men dismounted. Five men stayed with their horses leaving the tallest man to head on to them. He wasn't one of the men they'd met last night, and he had the stiff-backed authority of a natural leader.

'So I get to meet Mason Fox at last,' Luther said. He smiled, but then hardened his expression. 'But I thought there was to be seven of you.'

'There is,' Mason said. 'The other came early to watch proceedings.'

Luther gestured around them at the bridge and at the open gulch beyond.

'If you were concerned about treachery, you shouldn't have arranged this meeting in such an open place.'

'I prefer it to meeting in the shadows. That would give the impression I have something to hide.'

'So as you don't, the next time we meet it can be somewhere that's more suitable for me.' Luther drew the saddle-bag from his shoulder then underhanded it along the tracks so it landed a few feet to Mason's side.

Mason ignored the bag. 'Why would we need to meet again?'

'For me to pay you the rest.'

'There was never any talk of this.' His voice rose for the first time.

'It's a wise precaution when there's still a job to be done.' Luther spread his hands. 'And besides, if you complete the work to my satisfaction, the railroad will always have need of you again.'

'I'll remember that.' Mason dropped to one knee and flipped open the saddle-bag. He rummaged inside and what he saw there made him nod. 'We'll find you later.'

With that comment Mason swung the bag onto his shoulder and returned to the riders, who, without comment, joined him in turning and leading their horses back across the bridge. Luther watched them leave while Dayton contented himself with watching their side of the gulch.

Only when the men had left the bridge did Luther turn to him.

'And now we return to town to wait for news,' he said.

The unexplained meeting and the few enigmatic comments he'd heard had given Dayton a multitude of questions to ask. As he was sure he wouldn't get an answer to any of them, he beckoned Luther to move on ahead.

He looked around for movement, but when it came, it took him by surprise.

From the shadows ahead, Nelson Mann stepped out on to the bridge. He stopped in the centre of the tracks, set his legs wide apart, and considered the two men.

As Luther came to a halt, Nelson casually rested a hand on his hip beside his holster and smiled.

'Second and final chance, Luther,' he said.

Sheriff Cassidy Yates hurried along the top of Spinner's Gulch aiming to get closer to the bridge before the newcomers left. He'd watched the men until they'd stopped to speak with Luther, but as they'd been too far away for him to discern who they were, he'd decided to get closer.

To his annoyance when he came out on a high rock that let him look down at the bridge, the meeting was over and the newcomers had reached the opposite side.

He couldn't see this end of the bridge and he moved from side to side seeing if he could pick out Luther and Dayton through the outlying brush and rough terrain. But most of the end of the bridge remained unseen and the section he could see was shrouded in shadows. He slapped the ground in irritation then, doubled over, he scurried away aiming to reach a more advantageous position.

He'd managed only a few paces when he slid to a halt, the sight ahead surprising him. A man he hadn't seen before was blocking his way. The confident gleam in the man's eye said he had been silently sneaking up on him from behind.

'I knew,' the man said, 'that Luther would sell us out.'

'So you're with those hired men, are you?'

The man smiled, suggesting he was pleased that Cassidy didn't know many details about the meeting that had just taken place. He glanced at the bridge and moved as if to leave, but then without warning he briskly turned on his heel and threw himself at Cassidy.

His sudden action caught Cassidy unawares. Both men went crashing to the ground.

Cassidy landed on his back on the edge of the high rock with his head dangling over the side and despite the man bearing down on him he couldn't help but glance down. The drop below was sheer with nothing to halt his fall before hitting the rocks beside the river, 200 feet below.

That sight provided all the encouragement Cassidy needed to fight for his life. He slapped both hands on his assailant's shoulders and strained to throw him aside, but the man had a firm grip of him and Cassidy couldn't dislodge him.

They rocked from side to side with neither man making headway, but then the man raised himself and released a hand which he bunched then used to club Cassidy's jaw. The blow was strong enough to slam the back of Cassidy's head into the rock below and temporarily stun him. So heartened, the man drew his fist back even further for a second blow.

Through his swirling vision Cassidy saw the punch coming and jerked away from it, but that had the unfortunate effect of letting the blow hammer into the side of his head behind the ear.

His vision dimmed. His limbs went

numb. Unable to control himself he rolled to the side to land on his chest whereupon the man grabbed him from behind, dragged him up from the ground, then bundled him towards the edge.

Cassidy had felt queasy before he was forced to look down at the rocks below. In desperation he shook himself, bringing some feeling back into his body. Still disorientated he grabbed hold of the edge of the rock and planted his knees wide apart seeking traction to keep from being bundled over the edge, but inexorably his assailant shoved him forward.

Cassidy teetered, his upper body stretched and strained beyond the edge. He had but a moment before he'd be sent plummeting to his death, so he did the only thing he could, and stopped trying to prevent his forward motion.

He went limp and let himself be pushed forward to land with his belly on the edge. His head and upper body folded downwards to let him stare at the rocks below.

Thankfully his sudden unexpected action had the desired effect and his assailant went scrambling forward to land sprawled over him. With his upper body bent over the edge Cassidy ran his hands down the rock face and, to his relief, he found a small ledge on which he could plant a hand to provide leverage.

His firm grip stopped him tumbling over as, with his other arm, he jerked an elbow back into the man's guts. The blow landed without much force but, having a solid grip of the ledge, he also kicked upwards with his legs.

The man slid forward over Cassidy's back, then downwards. A scrambling hand grabbed for Cassidy's jacket, but the cloth ripped and then the man was unable to stop himself falling. Without making a sound he slipped away headfirst towards the rocks below.

He crashed into the side and then went tumbling, but before he'd hit the bottom, Cassidy was concentrating on getting himself upright.

For several seconds he stayed still while he ensured he had a firm grip. Then he ran his free hand over the rock until he found traction for that hand too. Carefully he levered himself up before he rolled over on to his back.

He caught his breath with several large gulps while rubbing the back of his head, then got to his knees and looked around. Nobody else was close.

It was unlikely that the men on the bridge had failed to see the man tumbling to his death, but when he looked down at the bridge he couldn't see anyone.

Then he heard voices. They were raised and sounded angry.

'So,' Luther Chisholm said, 'you've come for me again.'

Nelson Mann laughed with an exaggerated snort.

'You didn't think I'd give up that easily,' he said, 'did you?'

'Then why have you showed yourself

only after my meeting?'

'Because I gave you every chance to heed my warning. You didn't, but then again men like you are irrelevant. Even if I'd stopped you, they'd have sent another.' Nelson settled his stance, his small movement making Luther flinch and cast a worried glance at Dayton. 'And now you'll get the same treatment as your hired guns will get.'

With Luther's usual calm demeanour slipping away, Dayton got the hint that now was the time when he'd be called upon to prove his worth.

So while drawing his gun with one hand he moved to grab Luther with the other, aiming to drag him backwards so that he could stand in front of him. But before his gun had even cleared leather he was already too late.

Nelson ripped his gun from its holster and blasted a low shot into Luther's guts that made him fold over and stumble into Dayton. A second shot high to the chest sent him reeling away.

As Luther staggered towards the side of the bridge, a hand clawing at his holed chest, Nelson holstered his gun.

Dayton put the thought of returning gunfire from his mind and instead moved towards Luther. He put a hand on his bowed back.

'What can I do?' he asked.

Luther's only reply was a strangulated grunt of pain as his faltering progress reached the fence that bordered the sides of the bridge. There was only one horizontal plank and Luther threw out a hand to grab it, but then his strength gave way and he fell against the wood.

The plank creaked, looking for a moment as if it would hold, but then with a loud snap the plank broke and Luther went tumbling over the side. Luther was probably already dead, but in a reflex action Dayton lunged for him.

He grabbed a trailing arm and held on, but Luther had already slipped over the side. His dead weight dragged

Dayton with him and yanked him towards the edge.

Luckily Dayton's grip wasn't a strong one and Luther's arm slid out of Dayton's hand leaving him standing on the edge with one foot in the air and the other planted on the bridge.

Then he tipped over.

He had a terrifying vision of the dark mass of the river and boulders below with Luther tumbling away from him. He waved his arms, seeking to regain his balance. He failed and plummeted downwards, but then a flailing arm slapped against the broken and dangling plank.

Dayton twisted his hand and gathered a grip on the plank. To his relief he jerked to a halt, the sudden stoppage making him feel as if he'd torn his arm from the socket. He swayed gently before coming to a halt.

When he dared to assess his situation it was precarious.

He was dangling one-handed beneath the bridge on the end of the broken plank. The plank itself was pointing straight down and all that was keeping it attached to an upright post were two bent nails driven sideways through it.

Dayton swung his free hand up and grabbed the plank. He breathed a sigh of relief as he gathered a more secure hold, but then the plank creaked ominously. Dayton looked up its length to the post and was sure he could see more of the nails that secured it. Worse, the gap was widening.

He didn't wait around to see if he was right. He released, then threw up a hand to get a handhold a few inches higher, then repeated the motion. With all his weight suspended from his hands, his progress was painfully slow.

He didn't dare look up to see if the plank was still parting from the post, but as his eyeline drew level with the bridge, he heard a popping sound that suggested the nails were losing their hold.

He was just starting to plan how he would get himself to safety when, with a grinding of metal and wood, the plank split then broke loose.

The side of the bridge blurred before his eyes before he came to a sudden halt. He held his breath, unable to work out how he'd become snagged while not wishing to risk dislodging himself by making any untoward movements.

Then he felt a hand around his forearm and looked up to see that someone had saved him. He raised his other arm and this time gathered a mutual grasping of wrists. Then his saviour raised him and deposited him on the bridge.

'Obliged you came, Cass. . . . ' Dayton trailed off when he saw who had saved him. It wasn't the lawman.

Nelson Mann had returned.

'It was no trouble,' Nelson said, tipping his hat and smiling, 'for the man who stood aside and let me shoot up Luther.'

Dayton crawled away from the edge to the tracks.

'Why?' he asked.

Nelson shrugged, as if the question didn't need asking.

'My quarrel was with Luther Chisholm, not with a man who arrived in town in a freight car and looked as if he hadn't had a proper meal in two days.'

'Three,' Dayton said.

'In which case take this advice: never get that hungry again or you could end up working for someone like Luther Chisholm again.'

With that sage piece of wisdom Nelson turned on his heel and walked away.

'And thank you,' Dayton called after him.

Nelson merely raised a hand in a wave without looking back.

Dayton watched him until he disappeared from view in the gloom beyond the bridge. Then he shuffled to the edge and risked looking down. It was too dark to pick out Luther's body, but he was sure he would have been dead before he'd been dashed on the rocks below.

Then, after looking back at the other end of the bridge to confirm that Mason Fox and the rest had gone, he had nothing left to do here but leave too.

Feeling pensive after his brush with death, he took his time, pacing slowly along the tracks. When he came off the bridge he climbed over a rise then made his way to his horse. Before he reached it, however, he saw that his steed wasn't the only one waiting for him.

Sheriff Cassidy Yates was already there and he was holding Nelson Mann at gunpoint.

5

'We've definitely got them all now,' Eddie Bell said.

'We got all that came this time,' Jackson said, 'but the railroad has bottomless funds. They can afford to send more.'

'They can, but we can't worry about what might happen, only about what does happen.'

Jackson nodded, then looked up to the ridge with a forlorn expression on his face.

'And what did happen.'

Eddie grunted that he agreed with the sentiment and, feeling sure there wouldn't be any unexpected surprises, they left their house and made their way over to the ridge on the right of the gorge.

The last day had been fraught.

Although they'd thought that they'd

killed all their assailants, at sunup they'd seen that one of the bodies was no longer there. A tense period had followed in which they had traded sporadic gunfire with the missing wounded person who had holed up on the ridge.

When that gunfire had stopped, they'd waited for as long as their patience had allowed. Then they'd risked coming out to find him.

As it had turned out the shooter had died from his earlier gunshot wounds, but that had frayed the brothers' already taut nerves and so they'd carefully examined each man who had fallen during the assault.

Only when they'd matched people to the horses that had been left did they allow themselves to think of the future.

As they climbed up the ridge, that future felt bleak. They both expected to see Sherman's body lying on the top, confirming that the brothers' refusal to relent had cost them his life.

When they crested the top they

stopped to enjoy the view as they always did, looking up the thin gorge that had caused so much trouble towards the distant spire at Bleak Point. Below them were the indentations that created an X shape. Close by was the river and in the distance was the small blot that represented the town of Redemption.

They looked along the extent of the ridge, but there was no sign of Sherman. They had already searched on the other side of the ridge so they knew he hadn't fallen to ground level.

It was unthinkable that the attackers had gone to the effort of moving him. Eddie turned to Jackson, a hopeful smile on his lips, but Jackson was staring at a point down below, his face set grimly.

Eddie joined him and with Jackson's help, saw the arm dangling over a ledge fifty feet down. Sherman had been killed after all, but he'd not fallen all the way to the bottom.

There were numerous ways down to the ground, but the ledge on which he'd landed couldn't be reached easily.

'We need rope,' Eddie said.

'We don't have one and I didn't see one on the attackers.' Jackson shrugged. 'We'll have to go into Redemption.'

Eddie winced. 'That's how the trouble started the last time.'

* * *

'Did you see what happened on the bridge?' Dayton asked when he and Cassidy had returned to Monotony and Nelson Mann was again locked up in a cell.

'I missed most of it,' Cassidy said. 'I had problems of my own to sort out, so I wasn't in a good position to see everything. That means your testimony will be vital.'

Dayton winced. He had been worried that this would be the case.

The journey back from the bridge had been quiet, as he had wanted to get his thoughts in order before he talked with the sheriff. But he was still no clearer as to what he thought about the situation.

'It all happened quickly. I might not be much use.'

'Most people think that, but take time to think through what you saw. Then we'll get a statement written out.'

Dayton nodded. Then, as Cassidy turned away, he cast an abashed glance at the prisoner in the cell. Nelson looked up from his cot and considered him through the bars.

'I saved you,' he mouthed. 'Now save me.'

Dayton avoided reacting to that plea by looking away and joining Cassidy.

After promising to return tomorrow to provide his statement, he left the law office. Then he took a roundabout way back to his hotel room, mooching around town with his shoulders hunched and his mind whirling.

He was no clearer on how he felt about the situation when he snapped out of his thoughtful fugue and discovered that he was back in his hotel room and staring down at the road below.

He perched on the sill and considered the law office. Cassidy hadn't seen Nelson shoot Luther, but he hadn't seen him save his life either. Dayton doubted this final unexpected action would make the lawman release Nelson, but it did put him in a quandary.

He would now be lying dead at the bottom of Spinner's Gulch with every bone in his body broken if Nelson hadn't come back and saved him. And it was possible that the time he'd spent had delayed his escape and resulted in his capture.

Worse, piecing together the little he knew about Nelson Mann and Luther Chisholm, Dayton couldn't help but conclude that Nelson was a decent man and that Luther had been up to no good.

'So,' Dayton murmured to himself, 'what am I going to do about it?'

★ ★ ★

'Has the prisoner talked yet?' Deputy Judson asked when he arrived in the morning to take over from Cassidy.

Cassidy stretched back in his chair.

'Not yet, but he's had a night to stew.' Cassidy stood and made his way over to Nelson's cell. He walked slowly to give him time to notice him. 'Well, Nelson, are you prepared to talk?'

'I've still got nothing to say,' Nelson said from his cot, without removing the hat he'd placed over his face while he'd slept.

'You had nothing to say the last time you was in there, except I learnt plenty about you, didn't I, Nelson Mann?' He waited for an answer. He didn't get one, but he figured he'd made his point. 'So do I waste my time figuring out what you've been up to, or do you tell me?'

Several seconds passed before Nelson raised his hat to consider Cassidy.

'You can figure it out.' He replaced the hat.

'Then the way it's looking is you

gunned down a respected railroad man in cold blood. That's mighty serious.' Cassidy turned on his heel, not giving Nelson a chance to respond even if he'd wanted to. He stopped beside Evan's desk. 'I'll relieve you later this afternoon, and Floyd will take over this evening.'

He moved to go, but Evan raised a hand.

'Be careful,' he said.

'I doubt Nelson's got any friends out there and I reckon those men Luther hired are long gone.'

'I wasn't worried about them.' Evan paused for dramatic effect then winked. 'Sister Angelica is looking for you.'

Cassidy winced. 'Thanks for the warning.'

He went outside, checked up and down the road for the persistent nun, then hurried over to the hotel.

A search of Luther Chisholm's room revealed nothing of interest. He had left no personal effects and the room was so neat it might have been unoccupied.

Then he visited the station, but the

telegraph man, who knew most of the key railroad personnel, had never heard of Luther Chisholm and couldn't relay any gossip about him.

So Cassidy contacted the railroad office in Beaver Ridge. The returned telegraph was short and merely confirmed that they had received the news.

As this response didn't even confirm that Luther had worked for the railroad, Cassidy telegraphed back with the information that Nelson Mann had killed him. This got the confirmation he required as well as adding a new cryptic element.

The short response was: *Unlikely. NM is a trusted employee.*

Further enquiries around town failed to find anybody who had spent time with or had even spoken to Luther.

When Cassidy returned to the law office he was starting to think that unless he got a lucky break, he'd remain none the wiser as to why Luther had come to town and why Nelson had killed him.

Dayton Fisher slapped the ground in irritation.

He looked over his shoulder towards the bridge at Spinner's Gulch a half-mile away, but didn't feel inclined to retrace his steps and try again to pick up Mason Fox's trail.

He wasn't a tracker, he had to admit, and for that matter he wasn't an investigator either, as he could recall nothing about his charge that would help him work out what his business in town had been.

Despite that, the shadowy meetings Luther had conducted gave him an uneasy feeling. Although, when he thought back, he couldn't pin down any particular aspect that conclusively proved Luther was intent on malice and which might mean that Nelson had been justified in killing him.

The only course of action he could think of was to see if he could find out where Mason Fox had gone, but he couldn't pick up his tracks.

At a steady pace he backtracked, pondering on his problem. When he reached the bridge, he snapped himself out of his reverie to concentrate on making a safe crossing. He paced his horse onto the bridge, but then a flash of colour down below caught his attention.

He slipped close to the edge and narrowed his eyes, discerning the form of a body lying beside the water on the opposite side of the gulch; this presumably being the man who had attacked Cassidy.

It took him an hour to find a way down to the base of the gulch and another hour to pick a tortuous route beside the raging water to reach the dead man. The effort didn't appear to have been worth it when he at last reached the battered and broken body.

There was no identification on him, nor could Dayton find anything that gave him any clues as to who this man had been or what he was being paid to do.

Dayton sat on a boulder and considered him, wondering if his attempt to prove whether the man who had saved his life had been justified in his actions ended here.

Then the thought came that even if he couldn't learn anything about who the dead man had been, one thing was clear: the man had been a gunslinger. He had not only a tied down holster, but a derringer concealed in an inside pocket.

This man had not been a hired gun of the kind Dayton had become temporarily. He had been hired to cause serious trouble. Although Dayton didn't know who would be on the receiving end of that trouble, his motives had clearly been malicious.

Unfortunately the two hours it took Dayton to clamber out of the gulch and the subsequent hour it took him to return to Monotony didn't help him to work out whether that excused Nelson's actions.

When he rode back into town the sun

was setting and Cassidy was beginning an evening patrol. He joined him in a steady stroll down the boardwalk.

'Do you know why Nelson killed Luther yet?' he asked.

Cassidy shook his head. 'Nope. His lips are staying tight this time. Unless he explains himself, I'll have to view it as cold-blooded murder.'

'I guess you will, but I reckon there's more going on here than we both know about. I only worked for Luther for two days, but I was uncomfortable with what he was doing.' Dayton sighed. 'The trouble is, I don't have any proof other than a gut feeling he was up to no good.'

Cassidy stopped outside the now closed bank, a section of the boardwalk where nobody was around.

'I trust your gut feeling because that's mine too, but without proof there's nothing I can do to help Nelson.'

Dayton considered whether this was an opportune moment to mention that Nelson had saved his life, but decided it wasn't. This act didn't change the fact that Luther had been murdered and it was perhaps an ace in the hole he should keep back until Nelson's situation became more desperate.

'Then how can we get that proof?'

Cassidy smiled, presumably because of Dayton's emphasis on helping him.

'First, make a statement. Floyd is in the law office. Get down everything you can remember and perhaps something will lead us to the men Luther hired and the reason Nelson killed him.'

Dayton considered Cassidy's slumped stance.

'You don't look hopeful.'

'I'm not. It's likely that unless Nelson helps himself, he's looking at the wrong end of a short noose.'

Dayton nodded then left Cassidy to continue his patrol. As he headed to the law office, he walked even slower than he had done before, his mind whirling with conflicting thoughts, and one consideration stood out above everything: he was alive only because of Nelson.

No matter whether Nelson was justified or not in his actions, nothing would change that.

He glanced over his shoulder and smiled on seeing that Sister Angelica had seen Cassidy and was pursuing him down the road. While Cassidy concentrated on not noticing the nun, Dayton speeded up and looked for a mercantile that was still open.

Fifteen minutes later he was sitting opposite Deputy Floyd Wright in the law office ready to make his statement.

'Mind if I have a coffee while I talk it through?' he said.

'No,' Floyd said, pointing to the stove. 'I'll have one too.'

The stove was near to the cells and so, while he busied himself with the coffee pot, he caught Nelson's eye. Nelson returned a brief smile and a shrug that acknowledged his predicament while perhaps silently repeating his earlier plea. Dayton didn't respond and turned to Floyd.

'Has he talked?' he asked, lowering

his voice, but not so low that Nelson wouldn't be able to hear him.

'Nope,' Floyd said.

'That's odd. He should if he wants to get out of here.' Dayton cast Nelson a sideways glance, but Nelson had rolled back on to his cot and was staring at the ceiling.

'Hopeless situations make prisoners behave in odd ways,' Floyd said as Dayton brought their coffees over. 'Refusing to co-operate is the only control they have over their lives, so they keep their dignity by being awkward. Most snap in the end.'

'Do you reckon he'll snap?'

Floyd sipped his coffee as he considered the question then gave an uncommitted answer, but Dayton continued to probe for his view on the situation. The bored deputy welcomed the opportunity to chat and so the two men were drinking their second coffees by the time the conversation moved on to his statement.

Dayton noted that Floyd had drunk

most of his second mug then declared that he'd start at the beginning by talking about when Luther had first hired him. So Floyd collected paper while covering a yawn, then flopped down onto his chair.

'You write it,' he said around another yawn. 'I'll rest up a while.'

Dayton nodded. 'You want another mug to keep you awake?'

Floyd gulped down the last of his current drink, swirled the grounds, then shook his head and settled back in his chair.

So Dayton leaned over his paper and wrote down the details. Presently he heard deep breathing and then light snoring coming from the deputy, but he continued to write at a steady pace.

When he'd finished, he turned the paper round to lay it before the sleeping Floyd. Then he stood and went round to his side of the desk.

He poked Floyd's shoulder, but got no response, then rocked him to see if he could wake him, but the light push only made Floyd roll forward until his head rested on the desk.

He murmured something in his sleep and shuffled his head onto his arms to get himself more comfortable. Then louder snores rasped out.

Dayton still waited for a minute to confirm that the sleeping salts he'd slipped into the coffee were making Floyd sleep soundly. Then he knelt beside him and unhooked the ring of keys to the cells from his belt.

He stood and faced the cells, the keys dangling from a finger, and considered Nelson, who was now sitting up on his cot and watching him with interest.

'You saved my life,' Dayton said. 'Now I'll save yours.'

6

'Nobody wants to go to Bleak Point, whether it be to take those nuns or not,' Cassidy said when he returned to the law office. 'It's looking as if the only way I'll get rid of Sister Angelica is if I take her there myself.'

Cassidy waited for an answer, but when one didn't come, he considered Floyd then smiled. Floyd was leaning back in his chair, but he wasn't merely resting, he was asleep.

Cassidy walked quietly to his desk, meaning to awake him suddenly as an admonishment for having gone to sleep while leaving the office door unlocked. He reached his side and moved to give him a firm shove, but then stopped, a feeling of wrongness overcoming him.

He looked at the cells but couldn't see the prisoner. Concerned now, he hurried over to find that the door had been unlocked and the cell was empty.

'Floyd!' he shouted, 'what happened here?'

All he got by way of an answer was a rasping snore, and for the next minute he got no clear responses from him despite his increasingly enthusiastic shaking. Only when he resorted to slapping the deputy's face did the bleary-eyed Floyd leap to his feet in shock, but then he had to grab the desk to stop himself falling over.

'Nelson's gone?' he murmured while holding his head.

'Nelson has,' Cassidy said, eyeing Floyd with concern. 'What's wrong with you?'

'I don't know. My head feels like someone's hammering on it.'

'Perhaps they did. What's the last thing you remember?'

Floyd sat back down, then looked around vaguely until his gaze alighted on the paper before him.

'I took Dayton's statement,' he said, picking up the paper. 'But I can't remember helping him much. I was mighty tired.'

'Had Dayton gone when you went to sleep?'

'I . . . I don't know. I guess he must have as it looks as if he's finished it.'

Floyd rubbed his forehead again then reached for the coffee mug. He saw that it was empty then moved to rise and get himself a refill, but thought better of it and sat back down.

'You stay here and wait until that hammering stops,' Cassidy said. 'I'll round up Evan and we'll find Dayton.'

As Cassidy moved to go, Floyd shook his head.

'I don't reckon Nelson's escape had anything to do with Dayton.'

'Neither do I, but hopefully he saw more of what happened than you did.'

★ ★ ★

'I have to get away from town,' Nelson Mann said, sitting on the bed. 'I can't hide away up here for ever.'

'Be quiet,' Dayton snapped. He went over to the window to look down on the road. 'Someone might hear you.'

His angry tone silenced Nelson but in truth he was more annoyed with himself than with his new responsibility. He hadn't thought through his hastily arranged plan to break Nelson out of jail beyond giving Floyd a dose of sleeping salts.

If he had, he'd have realized that getting him out of a cell was the easy part of the operation when compared to getting him out of a crowded town without being seen.

In the early evening, the town had been bustling and although nobody had paid any obvious attention to the two men coming out of the law office, stealing a horse for himself and Nelson was sure to attract attention. So to give himself time to devise a plan he'd taken his only option and secreted Nelson up to his hotel room. But after twenty minutes of observing the activity outside he was no nearer to conceiving a plan to get him away.

Then the thought came that perhaps

this wasn't his problem. He'd given Nelson a chance and repaid his debt to him. He turned and while sitting on the sill, considered Nelson.

'All right,' he said, 'perhaps we do need to talk, and not about how you're going to get free.'

'Then about what?'

'You know what I want to hear. Why did you kill Luther? Why wouldn't you explain yourself to Cassidy?' Dayton waved his arms as he struggled to voice all the issues that he'd pondered for the last few days. 'Everything!'

Nelson accepted Dayton's outburst with barely a flicker of concern.

'Everything sure would take a long time to explain.'

Dayton waited for him to continue but he said nothing else.

'Then tell me the important details and prove to me that I didn't make a mistake when I betrayed Cassidy and broke you out of jail.'

Nelson considered him and when he spoke his lowered tone gave his statement an honest tone.

'Has it occurred to you that I haven't explained myself for a reason, and that reason might be that I'm protecting you?'

'There's no need to do that. I'd already put myself in danger when I accompanied Luther to the bridge. I can deal with whatever trouble you're in.'

'It's not the kind of trouble you need to hear about.' Nelson shrugged. 'You're a good man. If I tell you, you'll want to get involved.'

'I'm involved already. The moment you saved my life I became indebted to you and even if repaying that debt meant I'd get myself in this mess, I had to give you a chance. Well, you've got your chance, but unless you can convince me that I was right to break you out of jail, from here on you're on your own.'

Nelson spread his hands. 'Then I'm on my own.'

Dayton glared at him, still unwilling

to drop the subject, but unsure how he'd make him talk. Before he could think of another angle to probe him, someone knocked on the door.

'It's me, Cassidy,' the man in the corridor said.

For the first time Nelson reacted with concern as he shot a worried glance at Dayton, who didn't move, wondering if he could sit this out and wait for Cassidy to go away.

Then again, if he'd thought about the situation beforehand, he'd have realized that after Cassidy had found the drugged Floyd, tracking him down would be his first action.

Dayton pointed at the bed then did a jerking movement to signify that Nelson should hide beneath it. Then he headed to the door. He composed his face into what he hoped was an unconcerned expression, checked that Nelson was out of sight, then opened the door.

'Come in, Cassidy,' he said, smiling. 'I was planning on finding you to see if you wanted to while away the evening in the Golden Star again.'

Cassidy's brief frown before he matched Dayton's smile confirmed that something was amiss, but Dayton maintained his smile.

'Perhaps later if I can clear up a problem,' Cassidy said. 'Nelson Mann's escaped.'

Dayton winced before he walked across the room to the window, giving the impression he had nothing to hide.

'I'd seen that there was a commotion going on,' he said, looking down at the law office.

'Did you see anything untoward after you'd given your statement to Floyd?'

Dayton jutted his jaw to give the impression he was thinking.

'No. I finished writing it, but Floyd was dropping off to sleep and that made me feel tired too, so I left.' To tell a convincing lie Dayton reckoned he shouldn't elaborate his story, but when Cassidy didn't reply he continued. 'I'd not been sleeping well with all the worry about what Luther was doing, so

I came back here and slept for a while.'

Dayton pointed at the bed and the rumpled blankets where Nelson had been sitting.

Cassidy nodded and relaxed his stance, as if this response fitted in with his theory of what had happened. He glanced around the room then turned to the door.

'If you see or hear anything,' he said, 'let me know.'

'I will and good luck with chasing after him. He must be some distance away by now.'

Cassidy stopped in the doorway. 'If he left town.'

Although Dayton couldn't tell if his words had had a deeper meaning, they made him gulp guiltily.

'If you think he's still around,' he said, going over to the door, 'I'll join in the search. At the very least we should be able to prove he's long gone.'

Dayton wanted Nelson to take his comment as a request for him to find his own escape route. Then, still feeling guilty, he stayed quiet as they headed outside.

The next hour only went to worsen that guilt.

He accompanied Cassidy as they went around town searching buildings and asking if anyone had seen anything. Periodically Evan came over to report on the progress of his own search. Floyd stayed in the law office as he still felt too groggy to help.

The concern the two lawmen showed for Floyd only heightened Dayton's sense of the enormity of the betrayal he had committed. But he maintained his pretence that Nelson was to be found somewhere in town and he joined the lawmen in entering every building they could and peering down every dark alley.

As time went on the guilt lessened and he even started to take the search seriously. He hoped that by now Nelson would have made his way out of his hotel room so that he was actually in a position to be found.

The search had completed a full tour of the town when Cassidy approached the one group of people he hadn't wanted to ask if they'd seen anything. And the response was exactly as he'd told Dayton it would be.

'Why are you wasting my time with such matters?' Sister Angelica declared. 'There's only one thing on my mind and that's your earlier failing, which, even after three days, you have failed to rectify. We are still here and nobody wishes to help us.'

'Do you realize I have an escaped killer to find?' Cassidy asked.

'I had heard.' Sister Angelica dismissed the matter with a wave of her hand. 'Now how do you propose we get to Bleak Point safely?'

Cassidy set his hands on his hips, his irritation with the nun finally bubbling over.

'I'll do a deal with you,' he said, lowering his tone to a growl. 'If you can help me find Nelson Mann, I'll take you to Bleak Point myself.'

Sister Angelica smiled for the first time that Dayton had seen.

'I accept your offer to take us there. We'll be ready to leave at first light.'

Cassidy narrowed his eyes. 'You did hear the first part of my offer, didn't you?'

'I did. I will help you by offering prayers for your success.'

Cassidy snorted. 'I need more than prayers, and so do you.'

Cassidy walked away, but Dayton stayed, an idea tapping at his mind. He waited until Sister Angelica had stopped glowering at Cassidy's back and had turned her irate gaze upon him before he voiced it.

'Did you say that you want someone to take you to Bleak Point?' he asked.

7

'That's the best news I've heard for a while,' Cassidy said.

'And it's good news for me too,' Dayton said. 'I need the work.'

Cassidy frowned. 'You must have needed it badly. Sister Angelica is more trouble than most of the outlaws I've arrested.'

'I know, but it's only two weeks to Bleak Point and then she can do what she wants.'

'And you?'

'I may swing round to Carmon, or perhaps I might head for Beaver Ridge.' He smiled. 'If Sister Angelica decided that place wasn't for her, then maybe it'll be right for me.'

Cassidy joined Dayton in smiling. 'Then I wish you luck, if I don't see you again.'

'You will. There's still a few hours left tonight to search.'

'And there might be good news on

that too.' Cassidy leaned towards him. 'Evan went to check on Floyd and when he came back he said he'd had a hunch where Nelson might have gone to ground. He wouldn't tell me what it was until he'd tested it, but I saw him going off towards the hotel.'

Dayton nodded then looked away so that Cassidy wouldn't see him wince. He could think of only one possibility for what Evan might have pieced together, and if Nelson were to get found in his room that would be impossible to explain away.

Feeling pensive, he joined Cassidy in heading to the hotel to see what Evan was doing, but when they arrived, the deputy wasn't to be seen.

'Where should we look for him first?' Dayton asked, standing beside the front door.

'I asked earlier and all the rooms are occupied so he won't have gone in the hotel.' Cassidy glanced around. 'There's another couple of saloons down this way. You try the first, I'll try the second.'

'It's also pretty dark behind the hotel with plenty of clutter. Perhaps Evan reckoned Nelson was hiding there.'

'All right. You try there and I'll do the saloons.'

After a muttered comment to be careful, Cassidy headed off. Dayton watched him go. Then, with a sigh to himself, he went inside.

Nobody was on duty at the desk so he hurried up the stairs unseen. When he opened the door to his room on the first floor, he was pleased to see the room was unlit.

He was about to close the door, feeling relieved that Nelson was now no longer his problem, when he saw that the window was closed. The room was stuffy and so he moved to go inside and open it. He'd managed a single pace when a hand slapped over his mouth and drew him backwards. A kick slammed the door shut.

'Be quiet,' Nelson whispered in his ear, 'and you'll get to walk out of here alive.'

'It's me,' Dayton murmured from behind the hand and he must have been understandable enough as Nelson removed the hand.

'Sorry,' Nelson said. 'I'm edgy and I wasn't sure who it was.'

'You need to be edgy. Deputy Evan Judson is closing in on you.'

A gulp sounded. 'I sure know that.'

A match rasped and light flared, brightening the room. When Nelson had lit a lamp, he was wide-eyed, perhaps registering shock.

'Has he been here?' Dayton asked.

Nelson's answer was to point at the bed. At first, Dayton couldn't tell what had concerned him, but then he looked to the floor and saw the foot sticking out on the other side of the bed. He hurried round the bed to see that Deputy Judson was lying on his back, seemingly unconscious.

Dayton knelt beside him and located a red scrape at the temple. Blood matted his hair. He was breathing, but only shallowly.

'He came in,' Nelson said, moving round to kneel on the other side of the body. 'I hid over here, but he found me. We struggled. I punched him. He fell and hit his head on the corner of that table.'

Dayton glanced at the small table that sat beside the bed, seeing a spot of blood on the sharp corner. Thoughtfully he rubbed it away then rolled back on his haunches.

As far as he could tell, the situation had unfolded in the way Nelson had said it had happened.

'It'd seem that Evan worked out that I'd hidden you.'

Nelson winced. 'If I'd known you'd get into trouble, I wouldn't have come up here.'

Dayton had been minded to accept that Nelson needed to get himself out of this mess, but this comment along with the shock in his eyes convinced him that he needed to continue to help him.

'We both made some bad choices,

but we have to make sure this doesn't get any worse for any of us, and that includes Deputy Judson.' He pointed at the door. 'We'll get him out of here and I'll get him some help. Then you need to find somewhere else to hide while I cook up an explanation for my role in this.'

After only a moment's consideration Nelson slapped his shoulder, nodding and appearing pleased now that someone was taking control of the situation, even if Dayton had no specific plans that would get them out of this mess.

With Dayton taking Evan's feet and Nelson his shoulders, they manoeuvred him to the door. A glance outside confirmed nobody was around; then they headed into the corridor.

On the way downstairs Nelson told Dayton that he should implicate him in this attack and encourage Cassidy to work out that the assault had taken place in the hotel room. That would give Dayton the best chance of explaining away his role when Evan came to. This was such a reasonable offer that Dayton told Nelson about his plan to leave town tomorrow by escorting Sister Angelica to Bleak Point, leaving the obvious follow-up thought to Nelson.

'Then I hope you can get away.' Nelson considered. 'Can I come?'

Dayton shrugged. 'Sister Angelica knows you've escaped, so you can't come openly. I don't know how much spare room the nuns have in their wagons, but if you can sneak a passage out of here, do it.'

Nelson grunted his thanks then silenced as they'd reached the front door. Dayton checked outside that nobody was close. Then they had no choice but to risk going outside. At a brisk rate they hurried along the boardwalk to an alley beside the hotel.

Only when they'd reached the safety of darkness did Nelson stop. He lowered Evan's feet to the ground then faced Dayton.

'This is where we part company,' he

101

said. 'I'm obliged for your help, and if you can explain yourself and get to leave town, I'll try to leave with you. But no matter what happens, I won't speak of what you did.'

Dayton wished him luck. Then, as Nelson melted away into the shadows, he dragged Evan to the side and propped him up against the hotel wall. His breathing was more ragged than before, so even though he wanted to give Nelson as much time as he could, he didn't think Evan could wait.

He hurried out of the alley and down the road. Thankfully, Cassidy was approaching, so he hailed him while pointing.

'Come quickly, Cassidy,' he shouted. 'I reckon Nelson's attacked Evan.'

* * *

With Jackson at his side Eddie Bell rode into Redemption.

This was the first time the brothers had ventured into town since they'd accidentally visited at the same time as the railroad men were explaining their plans to the townsfolk.

The ensuing argument had become so heated they'd been run out of town. This encounter had been shortly followed by the railroad men arriving at their home, hell-bent on running them off their land.

The town consisted of a short main drag with a rundown stable, an even more rundown mercantile and several abandoned buildings. The only building that showed any sign of life was the saloon.

Redemption had sprung up ten years earlier as the scene of the first silver extraction, but when the main seam had been uncovered further north in the Barren Plains most people had moved on. But the town had clung on to life, serving as a stopping point for traders before they embarked on the increasingly treacherous journey up through Redemption Gorge past the Bells' home.

That steady downfall would reverse

when the railroad arrived, or in the view of Jackson and Eddie, *if* it arrived.

After glancing at the saloon to check that nobody had seen them, they went into the mercantile. The owner, Bill Samuels, greeted them with a warm smile, but that died the moment he realized who his customers were.

'The last time you were in town you caused a riot,' he said, staying behind the counter. 'What you planning on doing this time?'

'We didn't want no trouble last time,' Eddie said. 'We don't want any this time.'

Bill considered them then lowered his voice to a more conciliatory tone, presumably remembering that even if they didn't see eye to eye on current matters they had always been good customers.

'It looks as if the railroad men gave you plenty of trouble.'

'They did at that,' Eddie said.

'But not as much as we gave them,' Jackson added.

Bill sighed. 'Any chance that they

talked sense into you?'

'Nope,' Eddie and Jackson said together.

'Then you'd better buy what you need and leave before anybody else tries to talk to you.'

'That mean there's railroad men in town again?'

'Nope, but everybody else who cares about this town is.'

'In that case we need a rope, one that's at least fifty feet long.'

Eddie's voice caught as he made his request making Bill look at him oddly, but he didn't ask what he needed it for and fetched him a suitable length. After Eddie had looped the rope around a shoulder and Jackson had paid, they left, but Bill's warning had proved to be a valid one.

Five men were standing outside the mercantile waiting for them to emerge. They were all townsfolk or men who eked out a living nearby. They had also all been in town the last time they'd visited.

Miles Carter, the burly blacksmith who looked after the stables, stepped forward.

'Never thought I'd see the Bell brothers again,' he said, setting his wide hands on his hips.

'Never underestimate us,' Eddie said. 'Many have learnt that lesson.'

'The only people needing a lesson here is you three.'

The accidental reference to the reason they'd had to come into town made Jackson step forward and adopt the same truculent stance as Miles.

'We're not interested in nothing you have to say,' he said.

Then he turned to head to his horse, but as one, the men moved to the side to block his way.

'This time you will listen,' Miles said. 'We've put up with plenty of nonsense from you, so now we'll have our say.'

'We'll listen to you,' Eddie said with a smile before he hardened his expression, 'provided you listen to us.'

'We know what you want and it's not

what everyone else wants!' Miles snapped. 'The railroad is building a line from Monotony to the Bleak Point silver mine and there's to be a depot at Redemption. That'll change everything.'

'It will, and for us the most. Redemption Gorge is the only route to the mine. That means they'll move us on. They could have used a different route — '

'There is no different route.'

Eddie conceded this point with a smile.

'Perhaps not, but they assumed they could move right through us. They never even tried to talk to us about it.'

'Only because you chased away everyone who came to talk to you with hot lead. I don't blame the railroad for losing patience and deciding to remove you.'

The group of men stood in aggrieved silence until Bill came out from his store and joined them. When he spoke, he used a softer voice than anyone else had used.

'There's one thing we all know, Eddie,' he said. 'One day, no matter how much you don't want to, you'll have to relent. You've fought on and even if you're in our way we admire that, but one way or the other you will have to accept defeat. Perhaps it'd sit better with you if you relented at a time of your choosing.'

Bill's eloquent words made the men facing Eddie and Jackson nod and even lessen their belligerent stances and step back. So Eddie considered his words carefully before he responded.

'If we could go back to the beginning, we might have done things differently, but we can't and too much has happened now. The railroad men killed Sherman, and that set us on a path we can never step off. Even if we have to kill every railroad man who tries to move us aside, we will.'

'One down,' Miles murmured under his breath, 'two to go.'

Jackson rounded on him. 'What did you say?'

'I reckon you heard,' Miles said as he and the other men stepped forward, the previous small moves towards an agreement ending abruptly. 'But in case you didn't, I said: that's one worthless Bell brother dead and I'm looking forward to the day the other two bite the dirt.'

Eddie stepped up to join Jackson and dropped his coil of rope. The two men exchanged a glance and then without further warning, threw themselves at the burly Miles. Eddie went low and with a leading shoulder he ran into Miles then wrapped his arms around his substantial belly.

Jackson threw a high punch at Miles's face. Miles flinched away from it, but the blow still caught him a stinging blow to the cheek and with Eddie continuing to push, it was enough to topple him.

Then they both looked up, and it was to face the four standing men moving in as one. Only Bill stood back shaking his head as his attempt to instil calm failed.

Eddie and Jackson stood side by side and again took on all-comers.

Jackson felled the first man with a swiping round-arm punch while Eddie bundled his first assailant to the ground with a flurry of blows to the chest and face. But the other two men then moved in and were joined by Miles, blooded and eager for retribution.

Jackson ducked and weaved away from his assailant's blows, but Eddie wasn't so lucky and after getting in a couple of punches to the man's chest, a backhanded swipe sent him staggering away. He stilled his progress and turned to find that Miles had hurled his arms high. Then with a great roar, he charged.

He gathered Eddie up under one arm then carried on to gather up Jackson. Then he bent them both double and ran them towards the wall only releasing them a few paces away and letting them run headfirst into the wall.

Eddie couldn't avoid slamming his head against the store wall and fell, poleaxed.

His vision swam then dimmed and he must have passed out as the next thing he knew, he was being dragged along with the back of his head rattling against the ground.

He waved his arms trying to tear himself away from whoever was moving him, but he couldn't touch anyone and his vision was still swirling and disorientating him. Then he came to a halt and a firm grip clamped around his right ankle and drew up tight.

Slowly his sight sharpened to let him see he was lying on the ground and the rope he'd come to buy had been wrapped around his ankle. The other end had been looped around Jackson's ankle, although Jackson still appeared to be unconscious.

Two horses were being led towards them while the rest of the gathered people moved in to stand around Eddie.

Miles stepped forward with the middle of the rope looped over a shoulder. He looked down at Jackson and then at Eddie. He sneered. Then he passed the rope to two men who mounted the horses.

'You two are mighty keen to stay up in Redemption Gorge,' Miles said with a smirk. 'So we'll help you with a ride home.'

Miles stepped aside and gestured to the riders, who, with a co-ordinated movement, moved their horses on at a walking pace.

Jackson was still so shaken he didn't immediately realize what was happening to him, but when the rope that attached him to the horses grew taut then drew him forward he sure knew.

'You can't do this,' he shouted as he bounced and scraped across the stony ground, taking a long swinging route that dragged him past the saloon.

'If dragging you back to your home don't teach you a lesson,' Miles shouted after him, 'next time we'll drag you all the way to Bleak Point.'

Miles continued to shout taunts but the noise Eddie's back was making, scraping over the stony ground, drowned him out. Eddie looked around and he noticed one small mercy. His tormentors were maintaining a slow pace.

He shot a glance at Jackson. As far as he could tell, Jackson was still unconscious, at least sparing him from suffering.

Then, as the riders left Redemption, they speeded to a trot and Eddie stopped caring about anything but the skin on his back.

8

'Is it all right if I leave?' Dayton asked in the morning.

'Of course,' Cassidy Yates said, eyeing the three wagons Sister Angelica and her nuns had drawn up. 'You've been a lot of help, but finding Nelson is my responsibility. And that'll be easier if I don't have her complaining every time she sees me.'

Dayton nodded, but it didn't make him feel any happier.

Last night he had told Cassidy he'd seen someone coming out of the hotel dragging Evan's unconscious body. The man had got away, he'd reported, but he reckoned it could have been Nelson.

Providing this explanation had made him feel guilty, but Nelson had encouraged him to divert suspicion away from himself. So once they'd left Evan in the care of Doc Taylor, Dayton had volunteered that, as he hadn't locked his hotel room door, Nelson may have hidden there.

He had led Cassidy upstairs. Cassidy had searched diligently until he'd found spots of blood beside the bed. This had helped him piece together what had happened. And it was an accurate scenario, aside from missing out Dayton's involvement.

The subsequent search for Nelson had taken long into the night, but it had failed to find him. Neither had Dayton caught sight of him, so he didn't know if he'd accompany him today.

The nuns planned to travel in two wagons leaving the third for him. While he'd busied himself with checking that his new charges were ready to leave, he hadn't looked for Nelson, acting as naturally as possible.

It had been up to Nelson to sneak into his wagon. If he didn't, he was on his own.

With Cassidy seeing nothing wrong with him leaving, Dayton climbed on the lead wagon.

'In that case,' Dayton said, looking down at the lawman, 'I wish you luck in finding Nelson and I hope Evan recovers quickly.'

'I'm going to see Evan now. Doc Taylor says he was lucky that you found him. Knocks to the head can be bad.'

They exchanged a few more pleasantries and then Dayton moved his wagon off. With the two other wagons trailing behind, he headed out of town.

Only when he was five miles on and he was sure that nobody was going to follow did he let himself relax and enjoy the sight of the open trail ahead. That relief didn't ease his conscience, but he consoled himself with the thought that even if he hadn't wanted to get away from the scene of his guilty secret, he did need work.

Sister Angelica was paying him only a few dollars. Bleak Point was a lawless mining town and the route there was dangerous, but he doubted that it would be any more dangerous than

116

working for Luther Chisholm.

He still didn't know if Nelson was hiding in the wagon behind him. But he didn't let that uncertainty dwell on his mind and tried to relax for the first time since he'd arrived in Monotony.

That attempt was working when they drew up at noon beside a small creek. He whistled to himself as he jumped down from his wagon and joined Sister Angelica, who proved Cassidy's complaints about her were correct when she ordered him to be quiet.

Apparently the three other nuns, who until now he'd assumed were merely being quiet, had taken a vow of silence. Sister Angelica didn't want anything to disrupt their serene state.

So he sat on the side of the creek and cooled the back of his neck with a sodden kerchief while watching his new charges.

He'd never been in the company of nuns before, but they behaved in the manner he'd have expected them to. Except for Sister Angelica, who kept a careful eye on him, as if he were likely to start acting in an inappropriate manner at any moment, the Sisters of the Sacred Cross avoided looking at him at all.

Dayton had gathered that their previous guide had abandoned them after taking them for several hundred miles; even after a morning with them, he understood why. Sister Angelica's continual glares were tiring and there was little chance of enjoying any companionship with the other women — except for one: Cynthia.

This woman was the youngest and she wore trousers and a jacket that were too large for her, rather than the habits the others wore. She hadn't taken a vow of silence, but Sister Angelica tersely cut her off whenever she spoke. Although she sat furthest away from him, she often glanced his way and after confirming she was doing this, Dayton couldn't help but smile at her.

His action made her jerk away in embarrassment, but after a few moments, from the corner of his eye he saw that she was watching him again.

He chuckled to himself, then dunked his water bottle. When it was full, he looked at her again, but found that Sister Angelica was in his way and was glowering.

'It's time to leave,' she declared. 'We dallied enough in Monotony and I have a lot of time to make up.'

'I'm ready to leave when you are,' Dayton said.

She considered him, then swung round to look at the other women, her gaze picking out Cynthia with obvious intent. Then she turned back to Dayton and gave him a narrowed-eyed glare that conveyed more venom than mere admonishing words ever could.

Dayton didn't give her the satisfaction of knowing he'd seen her silent warning and headed to his wagon. He went round to the back and dropped the water bottle over the backboard.

Then he busied himself with needlessly ensuring the board wouldn't come loose while the others went to their wagons.

The nuns were ready to move on when he got the answer to his unresolved question. Shuffling then running water sounded followed by a relieved sigh.

'Can I keep the bottle?' Nelson whispered from within the wagon.

'Sure,' Dayton said. 'I don't know when I'll next be able to give you anything.'

'I need regular water, but there's food back here, so don't worry about that.'

Dayton glanced around the side of the wagon to confirm nobody was close.

'I'll do plenty of worrying. Sister Angelica never lets me out of her sight for even a moment. You need to be careful.'

'As do you. I can see enough to tell what's going on.' Nelson chuckled. 'And Sister Angelica wasn't the only one watching you.'

Dayton gave a rueful sigh. 'I don't mind that sort of attention, but with all those eyes on me, it'll be hard for you to get away. We'll wait until we're further away from Monotony, then I'll look out for — '

'Bleak Point is fine with me.'

'Bleak Point is two weeks away. There's no way I can keep you hidden for that long.'

'As I said, Bleak Point is fine with me.'

More shuffling sounded as Nelson returned to his hiding place, effectively ending the discussion.

* * *

'How is he?' Deputy Wright asked when Cassidy returned to the law office.

As a forewarning, Cassidy gave Floyd a long stare that made him bow his head before he provided the news.

'Evan's dead.'

Despite the warning Floyd still exhaled his breath then flopped down to sit hunched on the corner of his desk.

'He didn't seem that badly hurt. It was only a scratch.'

Cassidy sat beside Floyd. 'Doc Taylor said that sometimes injuries to the head don't look as bad as they actually are.'

Floyd slapped a bunched first into his other hand.

'Evan died because Nelson escaped while I was on duty.'

'Don't blame yourself. We'll catch Nelson first. Then we'll worry about the rest.'

Floyd gave a non-committed shrug then jumped to his feet.

'Then I reckon we should stop sitting around kicking our heels and admit that Nelson's left town.'

'Perhaps,' Cassidy murmured, still feeling tired after the unexpected bad news. He pushed Floyd's coffee mug around the desk, pondering, then nodded to himself.

Floyd considered him. 'I know that expression. You've had an idea.'

'I have, and it's not a nice one.' Cassidy glanced at the mug again, unwilling to voice the thoughts that were rippling around in his mind. 'How are you feeling today?'

'Not bad.' Floyd rubbed his forehead. 'I still feel queasy though.'

'Have you ever felt that way before after falling asleep?'

'Not without liquor.'

'And you've found no bumps or bruises from being knocked out?'

'No.' Floyd frowned. 'Sadly I have to accept I just went to sleep.'

'You did, but it wasn't your fault.' Cassidy shoved the mug towards Floyd. 'I reckon you were given a sleeping salt in that mug.'

Floyd jerked backwards in surprise then paced back and forth before the desk. He ripped his hat from his head then thrust it back on as the possibility captured his imagination.

'But how?' he said. 'And who?'

'I asked around. Martin Johnson sold Dayton Fisher a dose of sleeping salts yesterday.'

'I can't believe . . . ' Floyd came to a

sudden halt. 'Dayton was here when I went to sleep and he did make me several coffees. But I don't like the sound of this. Dayton's a decent man.'

'I know. Evan must have pieced together events in the same way as I have, except it didn't sit easily with him either and so he investigated on his own.'

Floyd stopped pacing as he put together the final piece of Cassidy's idea.

'Nelson could have stowed away with him and the nuns.'

'It's possible, but if he did, we know where he's gone so we don't need to track him down just yet.' Cassidy went to the door. 'I'll carry on investigating, but if I turn up nothing, we'll go and find him.'

Floyd nodded and so Cassidy opened the door, but then came to a sudden halt.

Outside, six men were facing the door. They stood in a line with one man standing slightly forward.

'We've come for the man who shot Luther Chisholm,' the man said.

Cassidy narrowed his eyes. 'And who are you?'

'I'm Mason Fox,' the man said in a deadpan voice.

Cassidy nodded. Dayton's statement cited Mason as the man Luther had hired on the bridge before Nelson had killed him.

'The prisoner has been charged with Luther's murder. His future care is my responsibility.'

Deputy Wright came to the door to offer support, although the odd glance he shot at Cassidy conveyed that he'd picked up on Cassidy's careful choice of words that avoided mentioning that Nelson had escaped.

Mason walked up on to the board-walk and with slow arrogant paces he stepped up to Cassidy. Two men flanked him while the other three spread out to consider them with studied contempt.

'We're not leaving town without him,'

Mason said. 'You'll face plenty of trouble until you decide that handing him over is less trouble.'

Cassidy said nothing, judging that now that Mason had stated his intent, he'd leave. Sure enough, Mason turned away. But then in a move like lightning he whipped his hand out backhanded and caught Cassidy a stinging blow to the cheek that sent him spinning away.

In a co-ordinated movement, one of the other men threw himself at Floyd, who scrambled for his gun, but before he could reach it, the man had slapped a hand around his wrist. Then with his other hand he delivered a sharp uppercut to Floyd's chin that cracked his head back.

Cassidy steadied himself then moved to fight back, but he was already too late. The third man had moved in and thrust a gun up under his chin. Then he walked him back into the law office and stood him against the wall.

Over his assailant's shoulder Cassidy saw that Floyd was receiving the same treatment while Mason approached the cells. He walked with a confident swagger, his hand already moving for his gun as he showed his intent, but his arrogance evaporated when he saw that the cells were empty. He rounded on Cassidy.

'Where is he?' he demanded.

Cassidy started to snap back a retort, but with a gun stabbing into his jaw, he reckoned holding on to information wouldn't be wise.

'You're too late. He escaped.'

Mason paced across the office to stand beside Cassidy's assailant.

'I'd heard you were a formidable lawman, but clearly I heard wrong. You let us get in here and now it seems you let a lowlife like him escape.'

'Maybe I only let you in here to see for yourself that Nelson had gone.'

'Nelson?'

'Yeah, Nelson Mann was the man who killed Luther.'

Mason snorted. 'And where do you reckon *Nelson* went?'

'I don't talk to people like you about things like that.'

'You know nothing, lawman.' Mason moved in to place his face before Cassidy's. 'Otherwise you wouldn't be here and you wouldn't have got so much wrong.'

He glanced down at the gun barrel to ensure Cassidy got the message that one word from him and the man would fire. Then he pushed the barrel aside with an outstretched finger and turned his back on him.

He gestured at the other men to follow him outside and without looking back they left the office. In a line they walked across the road to their horses outside the Golden Star. Within a minute they were riding out of town.

Silently Floyd and Cassidy watched them leave. Only when they'd disappeared from view did Floyd turn to Cassidy.

'Now that sure was an odd encounter,' he said.

'It was,' Cassidy said. 'But it's the

first bit of luck we've had since Nelson escaped.'

'Luck?'

'Sure. Mason Fox wants Nelson and yet he left town, and that means he has an idea where he went.'

Floyd nodded. 'Mason headed north, perhaps towards Bleak Point.'

'Yeah,' Cassidy said. 'The same place Dayton Fisher went.'

9

Cynthia was looking at him again.

Dayton tried to avoid meeting her eye, but then found himself moving his head to consider her. She didn't look away and they smiled at each other before he returned to concentrating on hitching up the horses.

It was now morning and the second day of the journey to Bleak Point was about to get underway. Last night had been quiet with the nuns preparing a stew without fuss. They had allowed him to eat with them, but only after he'd agreed to follow Sister Angelica's instructions to sit some distance apart and stay quiet.

Afterwards Dayton had volunteered to clean the plates and pot. Sister Angelica had, at first, declined, stating this was not work he should be doing, but when he had insisted, Cynthia had leapt up to volunteer to help. Sister Angelica had seen where this debate would lead and had accepted his help and refused hers.

Accordingly, Dayton had been able to pass on a few warm scraps to Nelson, after which he'd slept beside the wagon. With the night passing without incident, for the first time he started to think that maybe they could complete this journey without Nelson being discovered.

When the horses were ready, he went to check on Nelson, but found he had a visitor. Sister Angelica was facing him with her arms folded.

'So that there are no more misunderstandings,' she said, 'it is not proper for you to pay us so much unwelcome attention.'

'I haven't.'

'I will allow that from your uncouth viewpoint you may not have done so, but there is one amongst us who has yet to take vows and you are providing her with too much of a distraction. You will take steps to curtail that distraction.'

Dayton blew out his cheeks and offered his assurance with as much honesty as he could muster.

'I'll try.'

'I fear that trying might not be enough. On the way to Bleak Point you may be able to fend off whatever dangers are out there, but we may find that *you* are the greatest danger of all.'

'I've never been called a danger before.' Dayton offered a smile that Sister Angelica didn't return, then hazarded an attempt to find friendlier ground. 'This is none of my concern, but why do you want to go to Bleak Point? From what I've heard it's not a hospitable place.'

'You are right that it is none of your concern.' She considered him with her jaw bunched, but then relented. 'But we are going precisely because it is an unsuitable place. The Sisters of the Sacred Cross must be where the need is greatest.'

'I'm sure the need is great in

friendlier places too.'

'It is, and so I prayed for guidance. The answer I received was Bleak Point.'

Dayton tipped back his hat. 'I'd have waited for a second answer.'

His attempt at levity made Sister Angelica's eyes flare.

'One day you will face judgement for your scoffing.'

'I wasn't scoffing. I just don't know how you get an answer to a prayer.'

'My prayers are always answered in ways I need to interpret,' Sister Angelica said in a clipped tone, as if she were explaining something simple to a particularly stupid child. 'After my prayer, the next person I saw was wearing a silver cross and that told me I needed to be where the silver came from.'

She folded her arms and glared at him, defying him to pour scorn on her explanation for why she'd travelled so far. Dayton wisely avoided offering an opinion and so she headed away.

He watched her leave, but when he

set off to check the wagon, he found that her concerns were justified.

Cynthia was leaning against the back corner of the wagon, a playful smile on her face and her hands thrust into her pockets. She was tracing a pattern in the dirt with an outstretched foot: she was obviously waiting for him.

Dayton glanced around expecting to see Sister Angelica storming back towards them, but Cynthia had chosen the side of the wagon that kept her out of view from the rest of the nuns.

'You need to leave before anyone sees you,' he said.

'I do,' Cynthia said, this being the first thing she'd ever said to him. 'But everyone's busy, so this is one of the few times I can get away to see you.'

'Why would you want to do that?'

Cynthia giggled then pushed off from the wagon and moved around him, putting herself in view from the other wagons. This made Dayton grab her shoulders and push her back against the wagon, making her giggle again.

'That's answer enough,' she said.

'You heard Sister Angelica's warning. I don't want you to get into trouble.'

'I know. And it's nice that you care.'

'I do, but not in the way I think you want me to. I like it that there's one member of your group who isn't quiet or awkward, but that's all I like.'

'That's a lie.' She licked her lips. 'I saw the way you looked at me.'

'Perhaps, but that shouldn't interest you. I must be ten years older than you are.'

'You must be, but why does that matter?'

'It matters to Sister Angelica. If she knew you were here, she'd be mad at both of us.'

'Then I'd better leave.' With a smile still on her lips she turned on her heel and slipped around the corner of the wagon. Then she darted her head back. 'But if you want, I'll sneak off my wagon later when nobody is looking and ride with you.'

'Now stop that talk,' Dayton snapped,

advancing on her and raising a hand to shoo her away, but she skipped away from him.

Then in a lithe motion she placed two hands on the backboard and lifted herself up to peer into the back of his wagon.

'I wonder if there's enough room back here,' she said.

With no other option, as he didn't want to risk her seeing Nelson, Dayton grabbed her around the waist and dragged her away from the wagon.

'You are not spending the journey in there.'

She squirmed happily before he placed her back on the ground.

'I guess I won't.' She licked her lips as she anticipated his reaction. 'It's too crowded for my liking.'

Dayton winced, then jerked back to look at the other wagons and check that nobody was paying them any attention.

'All right,' he said. 'Stop playing games. What's on your mind?'

She stiffened then replaced her smile

with a thin-lipped frown. The firming of her expression and her new posture in a moment changed her from a giggling and foolish young girl into a harder and mature woman.

'After you've left the nuns at Bleak Point,' she said with an urgent tone. 'I will leave with you.'

'I thought you were to become a nun yourself?'

'That is what Sister Angelica believes. Every day she struggles to move me towards that path. She will fail, so it'd be better for us all if I left with you.'

Dayton tipped back his hat. 'That'll be hard. I don't want to get into trouble.'

'You mean you don't want to get into more trouble than you're in already after having helped a prisoner escape then having secreted him amongst a wagon train of nuns?'

'That's plenty of trouble enough, but I reckon dealing with you might be a whole lot more.'

She laughed. 'It might, but all I'm

asking is to get away. You can leave me at the first town you visit.'

'And let you fend for yourself? I couldn't do that.'

'I've lived on my own before. What do you think I did before Sister Angelica took control of my life?'

'I have no idea.'

She turned to lean back against the wagon and looked aloft as if she were recalling events. When she spoke, her tone was low and the most serious he had heard.

'I got by the only way a young girl can in a big town like Beaver Ridge.'

Dayton gulped. 'I'm sorry for you. I can understand why you preferred even Sister Angelica to that.'

'It wasn't like that.' She bit her lip while opening and closing her fists as if the memory was unwelcome and she was debating whether to voice it. 'One day the saloon owner made me go with this fat oaf, and he wanted me to do things I didn't want to.'

'That must have been bad.'

'For him it was. The older girls had told me where to hide a knife in case it went wrong. This time I used it. I opened him up from chin to belly.' She pointed out where she'd cut him on her own body. 'Then I ran with the whole town baying for my blood until I fetched up with the Sisters of the Sacred Cross.'

'And you agreed to take vows?'

'I did what I'd always done to survive: say and do whatever's necessary. I reckoned that saying I'll be a nun would keep me safe and get me out of town, so that's what I did. But that deception has to end.'

Dayton heard Sister Angelica issuing orders for the nuns to leave.

'That was a tough story to hear,' he said. 'The best I can offer is, I'll think about it.'

Dayton moved to go, but she skipped to the side to block his way.

'You'll do more than think. You'll take me with you or I'll tell Sister Angelica who's back there.'

Dayton firmed his jaw. 'That'll make life difficult for me, but I can claim I didn't know he was there. I'm sorry, Cynthia, but I'll make my own decision and that might be that you're better off with Sister Angelica.'

She glared at him, her face reddening as she considered his unexpected refusal. She stamped a foot then flounced round on the spot as she prepared to leave. But then, with another swift movement, she swirled a hand to her belt, then turned and thrust the hand upwards.

Dayton saw the flash of steel a moment before she stuck a knife up under his throat.

'Now what do you say?' she asked.

Dayton raised his chin to free his skin from the point. A warm trickle dribbled down his neck.

'You wouldn't,' he said.

'That's what the fat oaf said in Beaver Ridge,' she said, 'just before I opened him up.'

'In which case,' Dayton said with a pronounced gulp, 'I'll help you.'

*   *   *

'We're getting closer,' Floyd said, fingering the campfire ashes.

'But we're still most of a day behind them,' Cassidy said.

Floyd nodded, then returned to his horse.

They had followed Mason Fox and his men, confirming that they were heading to Bleak Point. But one day out from Monotony, Mason had veered away.

The tracks had still gone broadly north towards Bleak Point, but Cassidy had surmised that Mason had a specific destination in mind and knew of a direct route there.

Cassidy, though, was concerned only with following Sister Angelica's wagons and to that end he was sure the campsite they'd found was the right one. So far the wagons were still heading towards Bleak Point, but if his suspicions were correct, at some stage at least one man would leave those wagons.

'How do you reckon Dayton will explain himself when we find him?' Floyd asked.

'I'm not interested in his explanation,' Cassidy said with some vehemence as he hurried his horse on. 'He lied to me and got Evan killed. I'll arrest him and then book him and his worthless friend an appointment with a rope back in Monotony.'

10

'You can escape now,' Dayton whispered, standing at the back of the wagon. 'Everyone's asleep.'

Shuffling sounded inside the wagon. Then Nelson looked over the backboard. He peered around into the darkness to confirm nobody was nearby before he spoke.

'I'll stay here,' he said.

'But you must have heard what Cynthia said this morning.'

'I heard, so I'm not the only one who needs to keep his wits about him.' Nelson chuckled. 'Except I reckon my troubles with Cassidy Yates are nothing compared to yours with a young nun.'

Dayton returned a supportive smile. He had avoided Cynthia today, not that that had been hard, as Sister Angelica hadn't taken her eyes off him.

Now, with the dinner eaten and

utensils tidied away, the nuns had retired for the night and for the first time that day Dayton reckoned he could relax.

'You're right and for that reason you need to move on. She's unpredictable and I don't reckon you want Sister Angelica knowing you're here.'

'Then you'll have to keep Cynthia happy and make sure she doesn't talk to her.'

Nelson was maintaining a jovial tone and in truth this problem was less worrying than the others he'd faced recently, but once they reached Bleak Point, Dayton wanted an end to recent events. He didn't want problems following him such as Nelson's escape being traced to him or an unwanted companion such as Cynthia.

'And how can I keep her happy?'

'I'll let you figure that one out for yourself.' Nelson winked, then still smiling, rolled out of view.

Dayton sighed, wondering how he could persuade him to accede to his wishes without their chatter drawing attention. He couldn't think of a way, so he walked around the wagon to the opposite side to the nuns where he'd laid out a blanket and a saddle as a headrest.

Here it was too dark to see far so he shuffled along until he reached his blanket, then slipped beneath it.

A warm hand touched his cheek and someone squirmed against him, making him flinch. He jumped to his feet, a demand to know who was there in the dark on his lips, but the request died when he heard a giggle.

'Cynthia,' he murmured.

He could see only the outline of her sitting up. A slap sounded as she tapped the ground beside her.

'Who else could it be?' she said, her tone playful and back to how it'd been before she'd threatened him with a knife. 'Now get back down here before someone hears you.'

'Sister Angelica probably should.' Dayton glared down at her, but with it being too dark for her to see his expression, he dropped down to his knees. 'Get back to your wagon before someone realizes you've gone.'

'Nobody will. Sister Angelica may never once take her eyes off me while she's awake, but she sleeps soundly, as do the rest of the nuns.'

'Which means,' Dayton said, leaning closer, 'you can sneak back without anyone realizing you've gone.'

She cupped his jaw with a soft hand. Despite himself, Dayton nuzzled the hand and this encouraged her to lean towards him.

'I need to apologize,' she whispered. 'I threatened you and I don't want you getting the wrong idea about me. I can be nice too. If you take me with you, you won't regret it.'

'I'm not taking you anywhere whether you — '

She placed a finger over his mouth.

'I lied when I threatened you. I won't tell Sister Angelica about Nelson and I won't hurt you like I did that fat oaf in

Beaver Ridge.' She whispered into his ear. 'But if you want, I might let you do what he wanted me to do.'

Dayton gulped, noticing how warm her breath was.

'You don't need to do that sort of thing any more.'

'I know, but I want to this time.'

She leaned back to look him in the eye. In the dark he caught a twinkle of light in her eyes and despite the brazen nature of her offer, her eyes were wet, perhaps from tears.

He brushed her check and felt the moisture there.

'Why?' he whispered.

She wiped the tears away against his palm then gulped before she answered.

'That man I said I cut from belly to chin,' she said, her voice small. 'It didn't happen like that. I got the knife out, but I was shaking too much to use it. He got it off me, but then he was so drunk he fell on it and gutted himself. I was so scared. I'm not now.'

She edged a mite closer and,

unbidden, he lowered his head to her.

'And you should never be scared again,' he said.

He felt her breath on his face and he had to keep a grip on her cheek to ensure he met her lips. They were still a few inches apart when a cry of alarm went up from behind.

'What do you think you're doing?'

Dayton swirled round to see the formidable outline of Sister Angelica standing at the back of the wagon.

'We were talking,' Dayton said, surprising himself with his calmness.

'You have no business talking with her this late at night.'

'Cynthia can decide who she wants to talk to, and she wanted to tell me about her life and her hopes for the future.'

Sister Angelica set her hands on her hips, appearing lost for words, perhaps because nobody had faced up to her so confidently before.

Catching the authority in his tone Cynthia leaned against him. Dayton placed a hand on her shoulder.

'I have had enough of you and all the rest who have distracted us,' Sister Angelica said sternly. 'You will leave us and we will make our own way to Bleak Point.'

She held out a hand, beckoning Cynthia to join her, but that only encouraged Cynthia to grip Dayton more tightly.

'I'm not going,' she said beside his chest.

With Sister Angelica standing with an arm thrust out, Dayton reckoned she faced a test of her authority, an authority that was slipping away with every moment she waited and Cynthia didn't move.

She must have realized this as, with a murmured comment to herself, she turned and went around the back of the wagon.

Dayton and Cynthia were turning to each other in triumph when a thud sounded as Sister Angelica rattled the back of the wagon.

'Stay away from my wagon,' Dayton demanded, getting to his feet, but by the time he'd extricated himself from the blanket and Cynthia's clutches, Sister Angelica had released the backboard so that it crashed down.

'*Your* wagon?' she said as Dayton hurried round to the back. 'You appear to have forgotten that this is the property of the Sisters of the Sacred Cross. You will take whatever is yours and then you will make your own way back to Monotony.'

'You can't leave me out here. It'll take me days to walk back to Monotony.'

Dayton grabbed an end of the board and strained to raise it back up, but Sister Angelica grabbed the other end and, with surprising strength, stilled it.

'You should have considered that before you broke my rules.' With a determined swipe, she slapped the board back down then moved to climb in.

'Don't,' Dayton snapped, the urgency

in his tone halting her. 'I'll get my own things.'

With such an untidy tangle of provisions inside, Nelson ought to have been able to stay hidden in the dark, but something about Dayton's tone must have hinted at his concern as Sister Angelica glared at him.

She started to climb into the wagon, but hadn't quite managed to slip inside when a gun emerged, catching the light, closely followed by Nelson Mann.

'That's far enough, Sister Angelica,' he said.

Sister Angelica flexed her hand, looking as if she'd try to swipe the weapon from his grip. So to pre-empt the uncertain result of this action Dayton moved in to stand before her.

'Put that gun down,' he demanded.

Nelson considered him, then man-oeuvred himself out of the wagon. On the ground he took a backwards step to keep both Sister Angelica and Dayton in his sights.

'No,' he said, 'this is where I start

giving the orders.'

Dayton shook his head. 'You're not that type of man. Now lower the gun and we can talk about this.'

Sister Angelica glared at Nelson. 'You're the man Sheriff Yates let escape from jail, aren't you?'

Although Nelson didn't respond, she narrowed her eyes nodding to herself. Then she turned on her heel to face Dayton, her eyes twinkling as she mulled over the situation, but before she could piece everything together, Dayton took a long pace towards Nelson. He wasn't armed, but he was sure Nelson wouldn't shoot him.

He held out a hand. 'This is my last request. Give me the gun.'

'Or what?'

He took another pace forcing Nelson to back away beyond the corner of the wagon.

'Or we'll sort this out my way.' He glanced at his fist. 'I know you don't want to kill me and you certainly don't want to harm these nuns.'

Nelson glanced at Sister Angelica then at Dayton while backing away along the side of the wagon. Behind him, Cynthia came into view having slipped around the front. Dayton couldn't tell what her intentions were as she walked towards him, but Nelson must have noticed his interest as he started to turn towards her.

Dayton seized the distraction as his best chance and he moved in, aiming to wrest the gun from Nelson's grip, but Nelson snapped back round on his heel, his fist rising in a sharp uppercut. At the last moment Dayton saw the blow coming and jerked away, but he was too late and the blow caught his chin, snapping his mouth shut with a teeth-rattling thud and sending him spinning into the wagon.

He grabbed hold of the side, but that failed to hold him up and he fell to the ground where he lay, his senses rattled. After gathering his breath, he shook himself and looked up to find that Nelson was standing over him.

'Had enough?' he demanded, 'or do I have to knock even more sense into you?'

Behind Nelson, Cynthia was still advancing silently. She was only four paces away and her hand had strayed to her belt where she had secreted her knife. She was darting her gaze between his prone form and Nelson's exposed back while gulping, clearly preparing herself for an act she didn't want to commit.

Violence, possibly a killing, was imminent and so Dayton did the only thing he could to stop it. He raised a hand in a gesture of surrender.

'We've had enough,' he said, looking around and drawing Nelson's attention to the advancing woman. 'We'll do whatever you want.'

11

'Are we giving up?' Jackson croaked.

'Is that in getting up to the ridge,' Eddie asked, 'or our home?'

The painful shrug Jackson provided suggested the latter.

This morning they were more limber than they had been earlier, but the scraped skin and bruises would take longer to heal.

The riders had relented and not dragged them back to Redemption Gorge, a journey that would have killed them, but Eddie hadn't been sure they'd given up due to kindness. After being knocked out, Jackson hadn't woken up and so hadn't provided much sport.

A mile out of town they'd cut them loose, then warned them they weren't welcome in town again. Then they'd left them to make their own way back home.

Luckily, after Eddie had caught his breath and inspected his wounds Jackson had come to, then immediately wished he hadn't. It had taken them the rest of the day to stagger home in short bursts.

'We have to get Sherman's body off the ledge and give him a decent burial,' Jackson said, 'but after that . . . '

'We did show the railroad what happens when they take on the Bell brothers,' Eddie mused, picking up on Jackson's resigned tone.

'We did.' Jackson gave a long sigh. 'So perhaps now is the right time to move on, but we'll bury Sherman first. Then we'll decide what to do next.'

Eddie nodded and they made their way across the base of the gorge. Slowly they climbed the ridge, every upwards pace making muscles protest and reminding them of their treatment, so by the time they reached the top, both men were gritting their teeth in pain.

They settled down near the edge to catch their breath before they looked down and tried to work out how to get to their brother. They took the opportunity to look across the plains. Although Redemption was only visible as a dark smudge in the distance the sight cheered Eddie.

'Despite everything,' he said, 'I don't want to leave this place.'

'Neither do I,' Jackson said.

The response made Eddie flinch as he'd not realized he'd spoken aloud, but then the two brothers looked at each other.

'Then what do we do?'

'We do what the railroad should have done the first time they came: we compromise.'

Eddie nodded. 'We stay and watch the tracks go down. Then life carries on as normal, except we have a hunk of steel passing by.'

They smiled at the way they'd backed down, doing so in the way Bill Samuels had suggested of finding a way that was theirs and at a time of their choosing.

Feeling more contented they got up and peered over the edge.

This time they picked out the body without difficulty. Sherman was lying closer to the edge, his frayed jacket sleeve suggesting that birds had picked at him and moved him slightly.

This sobering sight made it easier for them to work out how they'd raise him. They agreed that they wouldn't go down; they'd attempt the less dignified method of lassoing him.

It took an hour and several dozen attempts before they steered the rope around the body's shoulders then dragged it back around his chest. Then they drew him up.

Foot by foot the wind-dried body rose up to join them and it was with some distaste that they deposited it on the rocky ground. Jackson began to wrap the body in the blanket they'd brought, but then stopped and knelt to peer at the face.

'Come and see this,' he said.

'I saw the state he was in on the way up,' Eddie said, curling his lip in distaste. 'I'd prefer to remember our brother the way he was.'

'And you still can.' Jackson moved back. 'This man isn't Sherman.'

'What the . . . ?' Eddie murmured then took Jackson's place.

Although the build was the same as Sherman's and the clothes were broadly what he'd remembered Sherman had been wearing, the man had brown hair whereas Sherman's hair was black.

Encouraged, Eddie peered closer and saw that the man's face had survived in a better state than he'd expected, confirming Jackson's belief.

'Our brother is still alive,' Jackson said.

Eddie rummaged through the man's pockets and located several letters. As he searched through them, he felt more optimistic.

'And he might still be trying to fetch help,' Eddie said.

'Let's hope he returns before the railroad does, then.'

'After thinking him dead I'll settle for him returning.'

Jackson grunted agreement then fell silent when Eddie identified the one name that was appearing prominently on most of the documents. It was a man he'd never heard of before: Nelson Mann.

★   ★   ★

With a saddle-bag containing a hunk of hard bread and a few strips of beef along with a filled water bottle looped over a shoulder, Dayton faced the distant town of Monotony.

After two days on the wagons, he judged it would take him at least twice as long to get back to town. He turned and looked towards Bleak Point.

The mining town was twelve days' riding away and it would probably take him more than a month to reach, provided he ever did, as he'd gathered that crossing the Barren Plains was arduous. Bleak Point was also the place where Nelson Mann had taken Cynthia.

That last thought decided it for

him and, at a steady pace, he set off following the wheel tracks.

The previous night there had been no reasoning with Nelson as he returned to behaving like the determined man who had gunned down Luther Chisholm. He had herded the nuns together, then forced them to set off with him despite the lateness of the hour.

When Dayton had confronted him, Nelson had abandoned him. Cynthia had tried to stay with him, and Dayton would have let her, but Nelson had given her no choice.

Afterwards, Dayton had stayed put through the night, not wanting to risk getting even more lost in the dark, and now at first light he faced a long journey.

Thankfully the morning stayed cool, but once the sun had burnt off the high cloud, the sun beat down on his back, slowing him down to a trudge. The terrain was barren and filled with low scrub that provided no shelter from the heat.

Only the sight of the distant mountains that contained the rocky spire at Bleak Point gave him hope that the journey would end, but as the afternoon wore on, that hope became more of a taunt.

Before the sun closed on the horizon he'd drunk most of his water and he didn't know when he'd next be able to find more.

The one thought that kept his spirits up was that despite everything, Nelson was a decent man who had acted through desperation. In which case he wouldn't have abandoned him to die and there would be water about.

Sure enough, as sundown approached he saw the welcoming shimmer of a broad river ahead. He speeded up to a trot, then broke into a sprint and when he reached the banks he hurled himself headfirst into the water.

He came up gasping then waded back to the shallows where he knelt and splashed about to cool down while gulping handfuls of water.

Then he took stock of the situation. The wagon tracks had gone towards the river and, as the river swung round to head north, he hoped that Nelson had continued alongside it.

Before testing out that theory he enjoyed a last few moments in the cool water and ducked down. He stayed underwater for as long as he could then burst back up and began to wade on to dry land.

Two riders were on the bank facing him, their forms hard to discern with the low sun at their backs.

'That's far enough, Dayton Fisher,' one man said.

Dayton raised a hand to his brow and narrowed his eyes, discerning the form of Sheriff Cassidy Yates. Deputy Floyd Wright was at his side.

Dayton couldn't help but look up and down the river searching for an escape route. There was nowhere to run to where the lawmen wouldn't round him up within minutes.

So he put on an honest expression,

spread his hands and smiled.

'It's good to see you, Cassidy,' he said in a light tone. 'I sure have a story to tell.'

'I hope it's a better one than the others you've told me.' Cassidy gestured for him to get out of the water. 'Because you are under arrest.'

'You've got me wrong, old friend,' Dayton said, maintaining the light tone despite his mounting concern. 'Wait until you've heard me out.'

'I'll listen, as will Floyd, but there's one person who'll never hear your excuses.'

'Who?' Dayton asked, getting an inkling of what had changed Cassidy's mind about him.

'Deputy Evan Judson. He's dead.'

Dayton had been prepared to talk through an explanation of what had happened that still avoided mentioning his involvement in Nelson's escape, but this revelation made his mouth go dry.

Worse, Cassidy's stern glare said he wouldn't have believed him anyhow.

12

'They're coming,' Jackson said, his gaze locked on a dust cloud on the horizon.

'The railroad?' Eddie asked.

Jackson gave a brief nod and without further word, the two brothers headed to their house to collect their guns. For the last few days they had licked their wounds and now felt strong enough to move around and to think of the future, even if they were unsure what that future held.

By the time they emerged they could discern that there were three wagons and that one wagon was moving ahead of the other two.

'If they're going to attack,' Jackson said, drawing Eddie's attention to the lead wagon, 'I wouldn't expect them to come in single file.'

'Maybe they're prepared to talk.'

'Hopefully, but we've survived by not taking chances.'

Jackson took up a position at the corner of the house while Eddie stayed in view. Then they waited with their guns holstered.

The first inkling that events might not turn out badly came when Jackson whistled happily under his breath. Then he laughed.

'What's wrong?' Eddie asked.

'I don't believe it,' Jackson said, stepping out from the corner. He pointed. 'Look!'

Eddie narrowed his eyes. His eyes weren't as sharp as Jackson's, but the wagon driver did appear familiar. His heart raced as the thought came as to who it was. Then, when the driver waved, he let out a whoop.

'It's Sherman,' he declared shaking a fist in triumph. 'He is alive!'

Jackson and Eddie hurried out to meet him. They pounded across the ground, their bruises forgotten as they enjoyed themselves for the first time in a week. They whooped with delight and waved before coming to a halt in front of the wagon and jumping up and down on the spot.

Sherman drew the wagon to a halt then jumped down to consider his delighted brothers.

'I never expected to get a welcome like this,' he said, smiling.

'We never thought we'd get another chance to welcome you,' Eddie said, 'that's why.'

Sherman shook both brothers' hands and then when they all thought that wasn't a sufficiently enthusiastic greeting, they exchanged pats on the back followed by a brief hug. Then, despite the initial euphoria wearing off, they all looked at each other while trying unsuccessfully to subdue their smiles.

'Does that mean I've been gone for so long you thought I was dead?' Sherman asked.

'We thought you were dead from the first moment.'

Eddie then brought Sherman up to date on events.

'I thought I'd stopped things from getting worse,' Sherman said. He glanced at the trailing wagons, which were slowing as they approached the house. 'I didn't know you were in an even worse situation.'

'It sounds as if you have a story to tell too.'

Sherman nodded then kicked at the dirt as if he were reluctant to voice it.

'I killed a railroad man too,' he said finally, 'the one Nelson Mann reported to. I thought getting the lead man would stop them, but he'd already hired guns and they could be coming here.'

'That's not your fault and besides, we fought off the last men they sent against us.'

'And,' Jackson said, pointing at the approaching wagons, 'you've brought reinforcements.'

Sherman winced. 'They won't help us.'

'What do you mean?' Eddie asked, but before Sherman could answer, the sharp-eyed Jackson muttered an oath that made Sherman provide a rueful smile then swing round to face the wagons.

Eddie looked at one man and then the other wondering what the problem was, but with both men watching the wagons, he turned to them. He saw that several people were sitting on the seats. They were black-clad. And they appeared to be women.

He narrowed his eyes and leant forward. Then he gulped.

'Nuns?' he asked.

'Sure,' Sherman said.

'Any of them useful with a gun?'

'Nope.'

★   ★   ★

Cassidy watched his prisoner drink, still feeling the same contempt for him as he'd felt when he'd first pieced together what he'd done.

'Obliged,' Dayton said when he'd finished.

He held out the water bottle and

tried to catch his eye, as he had done before, but Cassidy merely took the bottle.

'We won't stop again until we reach Redemption,' Cassidy said, then used the rope that bound Dayton's hands to drag him to his feet.

'I'm not sure they went to Redemption though.'

Cassidy turned away and gestured for Floyd to deal with him.

As they were aiming to make good time, they'd had no choice but to let him ride doubled-up with Deputy Wright. But as Floyd came over, Cassidy sighed, deciding that if there ever was a time when he should discuss matters with Dayton, perhaps it was now. He turned back.

'Why?' He used a clipped tone to leave Dayton in no doubt that he shouldn't spin any more tales.

'Nelson wanted to get as far away from Monotony as he could, and as he took the nuns with him, I'm sure he'll go to Bleak Point.'

'He might, but Redemption is on the way and he might leave them there.' Cassidy waited for Dayton to argue his point, but when he stayed silent, he continued. 'So why did he shoot up Luther Chisholm? And then why did you and he kill Evan?'

'He wouldn't tell me why he killed Luther and I wasn't there when Evan got hurt, but we did all we could.' Dayton took a deep breath. 'And before you judge us, you need to know the one thing I never told you, the reason I broke Nelson out of jail.'

Dayton set his feet as wide apart as his bonds would allow and waited. Cassidy reckoned he was giving him a choice as to whether he wanted to hear the rest.

'Go on,' Cassidy said, finally.

'Nelson saved my life at Spinner's Gulch. I fell off the bridge and I would have died, but Nelson came back for me and that gave you enough time to catch him. I had to repay what he did by giving him a second chance.'

Cassidy had begun to nod as he heard something that helped to explain Dayton's actions, but the last comment made him scowl.

'A nice story,' he said, 'except he used that second chance to kill a lawman.'

Dayton opened his mouth to retort, but then wisely he closed it.

Still irritated, Cassidy turned away and let Floyd deal with him. Then, at a steady mile-eating pace they resumed their journey to Redemption.

It was a well-travelled route. They were no longer following the nuns' wagons as they weren't able to distinguish them from other ruts, but Cassidy was still confident the wagons hadn't gone elsewhere.

They rode silently. He didn't need to discuss anything with Floyd. They had worked together for several years and they didn't need to fill the journey with needless directions and debate.

They didn't even look at each other until, in early afternoon, they caught their first sight of a few buildings in the distance.

Cassidy moved on ahead and in single file they trotted into Redemption. There were few signs of life. The nuns' wagons weren't here, but six horses were outside the saloon.

'The gunslingers?' Floyd asked.

'Could be,' Cassidy said.

'Shall I stay here and guard this one?'

'No,' Cassidy said. 'We stick together. He won't cause us no trouble.'

Cassidy glanced at the prisoner, and received a nod.

'I won't make things difficult for you,' Dayton said. 'I want an end to this with no more mistakes or bloodshed.'

'It's a pity you didn't think like that before Evan died.'

Dayton said nothing as Floyd helped him down from the horse, but when they grouped together, he looked Cassidy in the eye.

'When you catch Nelson, you'll work out what happened, but know this: he told me that Evan fell and banged his head. I believe him.'

As Floyd snorted in disbelief, Cassidy matched his irritation with a sneer of his own.

'Nothing changes the fact that the only reason Evan is dead is because Nelson escaped and attacked him.'

'And nothing changes the fact that the only reason Nelson had to escape was that you captured him, and he wouldn't have been in that position if he hadn't saved my life.'

Cassidy bunched his fists while Floyd muttered an oath, this line of argument being the worst one he could have tried. Then, without further word, Floyd pushed Dayton forward and they trooped to the saloon.

With his bound hands before him, Dayton filed in between the two lawmen. Despite keeping his prisoner status masked, the moment they slipped inside, the customers eyed them with suspicion.

These men appraised them from under lowered hats and their muttered comments made their colleagues who had their backs to them scrape their chairs round to face them.

Cassidy tipped his hat to them. Then the two lawmen nudged Dayton along to the bar.

'That's Mason Fox,' Dayton said when the bartender had placed a whiskey bottle and two glasses on the bar. 'Luther hired him. I saw him and his companions for only a brief time, but it was clear they were confident in their abilities.'

'I know,' Cassidy said. 'We've had dealings with them before.'

'And the fact that Mason's stopped here,' Floyd said, 'suggests he knows Nelson didn't go to Bleak Point.'

'Or he's already dealt with him.'

Floyd nodded. 'I guess we'll get the answer soon enough.'

Cassidy provided a rueful smile. Then, after taking a sip of his whiskey, he turned and held the glass cradled against his chest to consider the six men.

'We're looking for Nelson Mann,' he announced.

Mason settled back in his chair, a relaxed smile on his face.

'Nelson Mann has plenty of friends here, myself included.'

'That's not the way it seemed back in Monotony.'

Mason pursed his lips and the men around him glanced at each other and smirked, each appearing to relish Mason's response before he made it. Accordingly, Mason lasted out his revelation by standing and making his slow way over to the bar.

'You're right that back in Monotony I would have shot up the man who killed Luther Chisholm.' Mason stopped a half-pace from Cassidy. 'Except you got everything so wrong you still think that man is called Nelson Mann.'

'Nelson worked for the railroad as Luther did,' Cassidy mused, then looked aloft for a moment. 'You mean his killer took on that name?'

'Sure. Nelson Mann reported to

Luther Chisholm before he got shot to hell. The man who killed him is called Sherman Bell.'

'Obliged for the information, but I've never heard of him.'

'Sherman's not popular around these parts. The same goes for his brothers.'

Behind the bar the bartender grunted that he agreed.

'Why?'

Mason looked back at his men and gave them a significant glance that from the way they stiffened, appeared to provide an order.

'You're the lawman. Why should I give you the answers?'

'Because we're both after the same man and from the sounds of it, Sherman didn't go to Bleak Point with the nuns. Tell me what you know and I'll arrest him and take him back to Monotony. He'll be dealt with, and you won't have to deal with me.'

'That's a tempting offer.' Mason raised a hand that made the five men stand and move towards them. 'But it's not tempting enough. I have a bigger problem to deal with than just one man.'

As the men surrounded them, Cassidy glanced at Floyd, who released Dayton's rope to swing round and watch them.

'Last time,' Cassidy said, 'you took us unawares. This time you won't be so lucky.'

'Lucky, eh?' Mason stepped forward to stand toe to toe with Cassidy. 'The only person who was lucky was you when I decided not to kill you. Now scurry back to Monotony before I change my mind.'

Mason raised an arm aiming to point through the door, but Cassidy didn't let him finish the gesture and grabbed the arm below the elbow, twisted his body, then thrust his arm up his back. With a deft sideways motion he slammed Mason into the bar so that he folded over it.

'I'm not going nowhere, Mason,' Cassidy muttered in his ear. 'But if I don't get some answers, you'll wish that

I had. Now, where do I find Sherman Bell?'

Mason didn't reply and so Cassidy edged his arm up a mite higher and pressed him against the bar again for emphasis. But when Mason lay his head flat to the bar, he was smiling.

'Let go of me, lawman,' he muttered. 'This is your only warning.'

'I'm not — '

Cassidy didn't get to finish his threat when the other men took this as their cue to move in. Two men took on Floyd. One man launched a swinging blow at Floyd's head that he easily ducked under, but the second man ran into him and pushed him back against the bar.

Then Cassidy had problems of his own to deal with that stopped him seeing how his deputy fared. A man slapped a hand on his shoulder aiming to drag him away, but Cassidy elbowed him in the chest. The man fell to the side, grunting in pain.

Cassidy moved to draw his gun,

aiming to hold Mason at gunpoint and so end this fightback, but as his hand reached for his holster a second man grabbed his shoulder more firmly. In a co-ordinated movement Mason bucked.

The force bundled Cassidy away. As he spun he lost his grip on Mason's arm. Before he could still his motion, he walked into a round-armed punch aimed at his head. He saw the blow coming and at the last moment threw up an arm that deflected the punch, but the force was still strong enough to push him back into the bar.

There, he righted himself and with his feet planted firmly, he took on all-comers. The man who had tried to hit him readied himself then launched a haymaker of punch that would have tipped Cassidy over the bar if it'd connected. But Cassidy jerked away from the blow then followed through with a short-armed jab to his assailant's belly that had him folding over and coughing.

Then Cassidy slapped both hands

down on the man's back and threw him over the bar so he landed on the other side. He faced up to the next man.

He twitched away from the first aimed blow, ducked the second, then bobbed up and delivered a crack to the point of the man's chin that rocked his head back before he toppled backwards like a felled tree.

Heartened, Cassidy glanced to the side to see how Floyd was faring then saw to his horror that Mason had already subdued him.

One man was holding the deputy from behind while Mason had slapped a gun into his neck in the manner Cassidy had planned to do to Mason. Worse, Mason had adopted a casual posture and was watching Cassidy with a contented gleam in his eye that said he had been amusing himself by giving him hope that he could fight them off.

'Reach,' he said simply.

Cassidy watched the men he'd fought off get to their feet and move to surround him. Seeing no hope, he raised his hands slightly.

'There's still no need to make me an enemy,' he said. 'Help me and I'll deal with Sherman.'

'No deal. I avoid making enemies in my own way.'

Mason laughed then firmed his gun hand with a gesture that meant he was preparing to fire.

Cassidy settled his stance, ready to go for his gun or die in the attempt, but then a strident demand rang out.

'Wait!'

Everybody looked around to see that Dayton had made the plea. With him being roped up while the fight had raged, Mason's men had ignored him.

'Why?' Mason demanded then nodded to one of his men to grab him.

Dayton stood his ground and didn't try to avoid the firm hand that slapped down on his shoulder.

'Because I speak for Luther Chisholm now that he's dead.'

Mason narrowed his eyes. 'I recognize you. You're the man who was with

Luther and failed to protect him.'

'I was, but that doesn't change the fact that Luther was trying to avoid trouble with the law.'

Mason gave a significant look at Dayton's bonds.

'Seems you failed.'

'I did. The lawman's got some strange notions into his head, but it's not in the railroad's interests for him to die.'

'When the railroad hired me, they knew I'd do things my way.'

'Maybe, but you also haven't been paid in full.' Dayton raised his chin. 'I'm authorized to pay you the rest, but only when the job's done, and that doesn't involve shooting lawmen.'

This speech didn't get an immediate response as Mason sized Dayton up.

After the lies Dayton had told, Cassidy didn't know whether he was spinning a yarn to save their lives or whether he did have the money that Luther was due to pay Mason. But the plea achieved one result when Mason gestured for Dayton to be released.

When one of his men had sliced through Dayton's bonds, he rubbed his wrists then pointed at Cassidy.

'Now take those guns off the lawmen and we can talk.'

'You don't give the orders. Sherman and his brothers have holed up at their house. Nobody can flush them out without paying a heavy price. We don't want to get ourselves needlessly shot up, so you'll bring them here.'

Dayton glanced at Cassidy, who returned a narrowed-eyed glare as he was still unsure what his aims were.

Dayton gulped. 'If I do that, it sounds as if I'll be the one who gets shot up.'

'Perhaps.' Mason smiled without warmth. 'You have until sundown to return with the Bell brothers. If you don't, the lawmen will die.'

13

'It's time for you to complete your promise,' Sister Angelica said, facing Sherman.

'I will,' Sherman said, gesturing up the gorge. 'You're free to go and get yourself killed in Bleak Point.'

Sister Angelica waggled a reproachful finger. 'Despite your mocking, I will pray for you. Yours is a more difficult journey than the one we will face.'

'I know. But the people I feel sorry for are the miners.'

The insult made Sister Angelica give Sherman a harsh glare before she turned to consider their home.

'As you have suffered, I will forgive you that comment. Will you stay here?'

'Nothing can make us move,' Eddie said, stepping forward to join in their discussion.

'That's the only thing I understand

about you. Staying when there is no reason to is admirable.'

'There's every reason. This is a fertile area. That's why we settled here and started the Bar X ranch.' Eddie pointed around the plains then towards the river and finally up the gorge. 'We have water and land. The X will always be here and so will the Bar X.'

'What do you mean?' Sister Angelica asked.

Eddie pointed at the gullies on either side of the gorge.

'We named our home for the X shape.'

Sister Angelica considered the gorge, then offered the first smile Eddie had seen her provide. She cast him an odd look, then bade the only one of the women who wasn't wearing a habit to approach.

'Cynthia,' she said, pointing at the gorge, 'what do you see?'

The young woman wandered over, her shoulders hunched, giving the impression of someone who had wanted to avoid being noticed.

'The route to Bleak Point,' she said. 'You don't need to remind me, but now that he's no longer guarding us, you can't keep me. Once we get there I'll — '

'I didn't ask for another outburst. I wanted to test something.' Sister Angelica placed a hand on Cynthia's shoulder and moved her round so that she was looking up the gorge. 'Tell me what you see.'

Cynthia wrinkled her brow in a demonstration of not understanding what was wanted of her, but as Sister Angelica did not say anything else, she did as bade.

'It's rocky and the route looks bumpy.'

'Forget about the journey to Bleak Point,' Sister Angelica said with extreme patience, as if talking to a child. 'We might not be making it, after all, but that depends on your answer. Tell me what you see.'

This unexpected offer concentrated

Cynthia's mind. She opened her eyes wide and looked at Sister Angelica, but when she didn't receive any additional explanation she faced the gorge.

'There's ridges on either side and beyond the entrance it goes in and then out.' She looked from side to side. 'It does that on both sides.'

'It does.' Sister Angelica closed her hand slightly. 'And what shape does that make?'

Cynthia moved to the side so that none of the wagons was in her way, then shrugged.

'What do you mean?'

'If you were to imagine you were looking down at the gorge from the heavens, what shape would you see?'

'A cross,' Cynthia said instantly.

Sister Angelica sighed then reached into her habit and withdrew the cross she wore around her neck. She kissed it then looked heavenward while the other nuns nodded and moved over to stand beside her. Cynthia smiled on realizing she'd provided the right answer and with nobody speaking again, it was left to Eddie to speak up.

'A cross is an X. What's the difference?'

'There's every difference,' Sister Angelica said holding out her cross for him to see. 'I prayed for guidance as to what the Sisters of the Sacred Cross should do and I got the answer that we should go to Bleak Point. I doubted I was doing the right thing when we were abandoned, ignored and kidnapped, but those trials were necessary to bring us to the right place, this place.'

'What you saying?'

'I'm saying we are no longer going to Bleak Point. We have found where we need to be, a place in the form of a cross.'

Eddie glanced at his brothers who returned bemused looks before he faced the nun.

'I'm pleased you like this place, but there's a heap of problems you don't know about. The railroad's coming and they don't want us here.'

'That's a minor issue,' Sister Angelica said with a wave of her hand. 'Nobody will move us, and we have the Lord on our side.'

Eddie blew out his cheeks. 'We're going to need him.'

*　*　*

Dayton hurried his mount on towards Redemption Gorge. Already the sun was closing on the ridge, adding desperation to his flight.

He had no doubt Mason Fox would carry through with his threat to kill the lawmen, but what worried him more was the harsh glares Cassidy and Floyd had shot at him as he'd left. Clearly they thought he was selling them out to save his own hide.

Neither did Dayton know for sure that Nelson Mann, or Sherman Bell as he now had to accept, and his brothers would be where Mason reckoned they were.

Cynthia's fate, which had worried

him the most previously, now felt like a minor concern compared to the other things that could go wrong. But he relaxed when he caught his first sight of the gorge ahead. The nuns' wagons were grouped at the entrance beside a house.

He also saw figures moving from the wagons to face him. They were too far away for him to see who they were, but enough people were there to comprise everyone he had to persuade to return to Redemption.

He caught the glint of weaponry as they showed they were unaware who was approaching, but one person recognized him before the others did and broke into a run. The sight of Cynthia running towards him cheered him; he drew his horse to a halt and jumped down.

She leapt into his arms and he swung her round, surprising himself with how pleased he was to see her. But when he caught sight of the distant form of the glowering Sister Angelica along with

Sherman and, he assumed, his brothers, he put her down.

'Did Sherman harm you?' he asked.

'No. He had a reason for taking us and it was a good one.' She considered him. 'So before you do anything you'll regret, let him explain himself.'

'He doesn't need to explain. I've heard everything, and he needs to be the one who listens.'

He wrapped an arm around her shoulders. Then together they headed on to the others. As they approached, Sister Angelica's gaze bored into them, but he didn't remove his arm and instead faced the brothers. When he stopped, Sherman spread his hands.

'I'm sorry you still got involved,' he said. 'I tried to avoid that.'

'Then you didn't do it very well, *Sherman.*'

Sherman winced. 'If you've been talking to Redemption's townsfolk, you have to hear our side too.'

Dayton glanced at the sun, now a fraction above the ridge. It was several hundred feet high, so he judged they had around two hours to sundown. But with the time it'd take to get them organized and then return, he didn't have long to persuade them to come.

'I don't care about your side. All that matters is that you come to Redemption with me.'

Sherman glanced at his brothers, who snorted while shaking their heads.

'We won't. We stay here where nobody can drive us away. We all agree on that.' Dayton pointed at Sister Angelica. 'Even she agrees.'

She folded her arms in her usual obstructive display.

'The Sisters of the Sacred Cross,' she said, 'have decided to make this place our new home. The brothers have accepted that and so we will not be moved on no matter who tries to drive us away.'

'You have no choice,' Dayton said. 'Mason Fox, the man Luther Chisholm hired, is here with five gunslingers.'

Sherman nodded. 'We expected that.

But we saw off the others they sent. We'll hole up and see them off too.'

'Even if you stayed to fight, I'm not sure you'd prevail, but we'll never find that out. You have to go to Redemption. Mason is holding Sheriff Yates and Deputy Wright. Unless you're there by sundown, he'll kill them.'

This revelation took some of the truculence from the postures of Sherman and his brothers and they looked at each other in a worried manner.

'We never meant for others to get dragged into this,' Sherman said.

'But we never asked anyone to,' one brother said, to a supportive grunt from the other brother. 'If they got themselves involved, that has nothing to do with us.'

'I'm not lying to you,' Dayton said, 'going to town will be dangerous, but you can't let innocent men die.'

'I understand,' Sherman said, 'but my brothers are determined in this. Going to town is too risky when we can prevail here.'

'But no matter what the risk, it's the only way you can save yourself.' As this was the only leverage Dayton reckoned he had, he moved forward to stand before Sherman. He didn't continue immediately ensuring he had everyone's attention. When he spoke he lowered his voice. 'Deputy Evan Judson died.'

Sherman winced and his brothers demanded to know who this man was, but Sherman raised a hand, silencing them.

'That's unfortunate, but I never aimed to harm him.' Sherman set his feet wide apart to show that this was his final word. 'So no matter what happened to him and no matter what will happen to the lawmen, we're not going into town to die.'

With the brothers matching Sherman's determined stance, Dayton could think of nothing to say in response and it was left to Sister Angelica to respond.

'In that case,' she said, 'I will talk sense into this Mason Fox.'

Dayton stared at her, incredulous.

'That'll never work.'

'I intend to settle here. So this is an ideal opportunity for me to show you there are ways to sort out problems other than at the end of a gun.'

She glared at the gathered men, defying them to say she couldn't resolve this situation.

'Then,' Dayton said, 'I guess I'll join you in getting myself killed in Redemption.'

14

'You didn't need to come,' Dayton said to Cynthia when he first caught sight of Redemption ahead.

'I'm not leaving your side ever again,' Cynthia said.

'I'd prefer to know you were safe.'

'I'm sure you would, but I can take care of myself and besides, if we're to have any chance of making this work, I have to be here.'

Dayton frowned. They'd had this debate before she'd got on the wagon and again after they'd set off. He'd failed to get her to agree the previous times. This time would be the last chance.

'Mason knows about the nuns,' he said, 'so they had to come, but not you.'

Cynthia sighed, lost for a new argument, leaving Sister Angelica, sitting on the other side of the seat to speak up.

'Cynthia is in control of her own

future,' she declared. 'It is for her to choose her own path.'

'Yes,' Dayton said, turning to her. 'It is.'

Sister Angelica narrowed her eyes, acknowledging she had understood that he had placed a different interpretation on her words.

'She will choose the right way, as we all have.' She glanced into the back of the wagon where the silent nuns were sitting with their heads bowed.

'I just hope you can be persuasive enough with Mason to let her live and make that choice.'

'I will. When I've decided what I'm doing, nobody stands in my way.'

Dayton limited himself to providing a rueful grunt then looked ahead at the approaching town. The sun was casting long shadows from the buildings meaning Mason Fox would be getting edgy.

Nobody was outside so Dayton presumed that Mason and the gun-slingers had stayed in the saloon. He trundled the wagon past the stables, aiming to pull up outside the saloon so as not to give them too much warning about what was about to happen.

'Then you'd better get that cross ready,' Dayton said as he saw someone looking through the saloon window. 'We'll need its protection any moment now.'

★   ★   ★

'Is that Dayton returning?' Floyd whispered to Cassidy.

'I'd be surprised,' Cassidy whispered back. 'I reckon that rat will run.'

Mason barked out orders for everyone to take up positions around the saloon, so the nearest gunslinger grunted at them to be quiet before he moved away.

Not that they had anything to worry about by letting them speak. The lawmen had been frisked and disarmed then tied together with coils of rope and left sitting back to back on the floor beside the bar. With no way to fight back they'd been ignored, but with the situation about to reach an end, one way or the other, they needed to do whatever they could to save themselves.

Accordingly, Cassidy wriggled, seeing if he could free himself from his bonds, but his hands were tied securely behind his back and his struggling only succeeded in grinding the ropes into his wrists.

'There's nothing we can do,' Floyd said, 'but hope that Dayton does have a conscience.'

Although Cassidy shook his head, something was happening outside. Even if he couldn't tell what was causing the consternation, he could see that Mason was acting in an animated manner as he stood in the centre of the saloon facing the door.

Two men flanked the door while others took up positions around the saloon. The man who was looking through the window snorted.

'Dayton's double-crossed us,' he said.

'He's not brought the Bell brothers back.'

'I'm not surprised.' Mason strained his neck to consider his limited view through the window. 'But I thought I saw people with him.'

'You did!' the man said with a cryptic smirk.

'Explain,' Mason muttered.

'You'll see,' the man said, then laughed.

Over at the end of the bar, Cassidy didn't feel like laughing. His worst fears had been realized and now his only hope was that Mason's threat had been a hollow one. That hope fled when Mason turned on his heel to cast him a narrow-eyed glare.

'Dayton gets to explain himself before he dies,' he said. 'Then you two will follow him before we go and wipe out the Bell brothers.'

Cassidy limited himself to glaring at Mason until footfalls sounded on the boardwalk. They all looked to the door to see what had amused the man at the

201

window, and the answer was one Cassidy hadn't expected.

Sister Angelica walked in followed by Dayton and Cynthia. Then the three silent nuns shuffled into the doorway to stand with their cowled faces downcast. Sister Angelica met Mason's gaze and favoured him with the same type of withering glare she'd given Cassidy on numerous occasions.

In different circumstances Cassidy would have pitied Mason.

'You'll be Mason Fox,' Sister Angelica said.

'I am,' Mason said, with a snort of laughter in his tone.

He gestured to one of his gunslingers to take Dayton's gun and to frisk Cynthia. The man found nothing, but when he moved towards Sister Angelica, she gave him an icy scowl that made him look at Mason for confirmation. He shook his head with a smile on his lips, but that didn't change her stern expression.

'I find nothing amusing about having

to set foot in such an unholy place,' she declared, considering the room with a disdainful eye. 'But if I'm to end this situation, it appears I have no choice. So you will release the lawmen. Then you will return to Monotony and deliver a message to the railroad.'

Mason spread his hands. 'Any other demands?'

'Before you leave, a contribution to the coffers of the Sisters of the Sacred Cross would not go amiss to help absolve you of some of your misdemeanours.'

'I'll be sure to do that.' Mason looked past Sister Angelica at Dayton. 'But first I want to hear why this one has failed in his mission.'

'He has not failed,' Sister Angelica said before Dayton could answer. 'I didn't give him an alternative. Keeping you and the Bell brothers apart was the only option I had to avoid unnecessary bloodshed.'

'Do you ever shut up?' Mason muttered, his tone now irritated.

'Not while we have outstanding matters to resolve and your rudeness is not making that easy.'

Mason looked at each of his men in turn, noting their pursed lips as they tried to avoid finding the situation funny until they knew how he'd react.

Then he threw back his head and roared with laughter. This encouraged everyone to laugh. When Sister Angelica looked around, favouring everyone with one of her annoyed looks, that only went to make everyone roar even louder.

By degrees the mirth petered out and while still offering the occasional chuckle, Mason went over to her.

'You're a funny lady and I'm obliged you came to amuse us, but now you need to leave. I've got business with Dayton and things are about to get ugly.'

'I am here to stop things getting ugly.'

'You failed, and you're also trying my patience. Leave before I stop finding you amusing.'

'Is that your final word on the matter?'

'It is.'

Sister Angelica backed away for a half-pace and spread her hands.

'Then I tried my best and I am truly sorry for what is about to happen. May God rest your soul.'

She moved to go past Mason and towards Cassidy and Floyd. Mason watched her in bemusement then grabbed her arm as she passed.

'You are not going anywhere but out the door.'

'Unhand me,' she demanded, but Mason ignored her and gestured for his men to seize the other women.

'Take them outside,' he said, 'but leave Dayton here.'

The two men by the door moved in to flank the three silent nuns, women who Cassidy had never heard speak or do anything but meekly follow Sister Angelica. They were standing with their heads bowed, their faces hidden.

None of them had reacted to the

events in the saloon and so the men treated them with some deference. One man pointed to the door while the other tapped the nearest nun's shoulder.

'Just go,' he said.

He didn't get a response, so after exchanging an exasperated look with the other man, he grabbed the nun's shoulder and moved to escort her out. She stood her ground and shook him off.

'Get them out of here,' Mason demanded. 'Carry them if you have to.'

'I could try,' one man said, 'but they look heavy.'

'And ugly,' the other man muttered as the nuns slowly raised their heads.

Open-mouthed shock registered on both men's faces. They scrambled for their guns, but were too late.

An explosion of gunfire tore out, accompanied by flashes of light as lead ripped out from the nuns' habits.

Sitting in a position where he couldn't see everything that was happening, Cassidy thought for one terrible moment that the men had shot the nuns.

Then the men fell away and he understood the deception everyone had expertly put together. The Bell brothers had disguised themselves as the silent nuns.

With the remaining four gunslingers getting their wits about them, the brothers wisely beat a hasty retreat through the door closely followed by a peppering of lead into the swinging batwings.

Dayton and Cynthia couldn't get out in time so they scrambled into hiding behind a table while with Mason releasing his grip of Sister Angelica's arm, she hurried on to Cassidy and Floyd. Mason ignored her as he barked out instructions for his men to get the brothers.

She knelt beside them, gave Cassidy a stern look that warned him to be quiet, then produced a knife from under her habit. With several quick slashes, she cut through the ropes around their chests. Then Cassidy rocked forward to let her reach their hands.

She worked quickly and Cassidy felt a couple of sharp pains as the knife jabbed his wrist and hands, but he was more grateful that she removed the ropes efficiently. Then they crawled into hiding behind the side of the bar.

'Stay hidden and out of trouble,' he whispered to her while patting her shoulder.

'Do you think I'd ever do that?' she said.

Cassidy gave her a rueful smile but she didn't complain when Floyd took the knife off her. Then Cassidy risked looking out to see what was happening.

Two gunmen had taken up positions beside the window and were peering outside at an angle towards the door. This gave Cassidy the impression the brothers had stayed by the saloon wall where they'd been pinned down. Mason and one other man had their backs to him standing beside the bar.

Cassidy jerked back out of view

before any of them happened to see them, but his motion must have attracted attention, as Mason snapped out an order.

'Cassidy's gone,' he said, 'fetch him.'

Footfalls sounded, closing in on the bar. While Sister Angelica pushed the ropes behind the bar, Cassidy beckoned Floyd to join him in adopting the pose they'd had previously of them sitting back to back.

Accordingly when the man appeared, he didn't expect that they'd been freed; he bent down to grab Cassidy's shoulder and drag him and Floyd back into the main saloon area. Then his eyes alighted on his chest and the lack of binding ropes.

'What the . . . ?' he murmured, then was cut off as Cassidy's fist connected squarely with his nose.

The man reeled backwards into the bar. Before he could right himself, Floyd was on his feet and pushing the knife against the man's throat. A moment later Cassidy had disarmed him. With a gun in hand he bade Sister Angelica to stay down and Floyd to keep their captive subdued.

He knelt and shuffled to the edge of the bar aiming to take on Mason's men, but Mason had heard the commotion and the moment he started to move out, lead ripped into the side of the bar spraying splinters.

In the main saloon area more gunfire ripped out and a window smashed, followed by another exchange of gunfire. Cassidy reckoned the brothers were making an assault on the saloon and so he edged to the side.

The saloon swung into view, but only far enough to let the first guntoter by the window appear. The man was firing through the window and not paying him attention, so Cassidy took a bead on him.

He fired, but the gunshot ripped into the window frame beside the man's head. The guntoter turned and picked out Cassidy with uncanny speed then swung his gun towards him.

Lead whistled by Cassidy's face so closely he felt a gnat's bite on his cheek, but he resisted the urge to slip back into hiding and fired again. This time his shot was more accurate and the lead cannoned into the man's chest.

The man staggered for a pace. Then another shot, presumably from the brothers, tore into him and sent him tumbling backwards into the wall, where he stood propped up before sliding down to the floor.

That left Mason and one gunslinger. Heartened, Cassidy moved out from the bar and saw that the brothers hadn't ventured inside but were taking it in turns to fire through the doorway.

Mason and the other man were trading gunfire with them.

Then, in a blur of motion, Dayton came running out, doubled over, from behind the table he and Cynthia had hidden behind. He dived to the timbers and slid across the floor to bundle into the fallen gunslinger.

Gunfire splattered into the timbers

behind him and at least one bullet tore into the dead gunslinger, but not before Dayton had slapped a hand on the man's gun. He turned it round in his grip and, with deft skill, blasted lead at the man who was shooting at him.

From outside Cassidy's view a cry went up followed by the sound of a body crashing to the floor. This encouraged the brothers to edge into the doorway to take on Mason, who backed away, seeking to take refuge behind the table from where Dayton had fled.

His action spooked Cynthia. She jumped to her feet and made to run for the door and safety.

Mason loosed off a wild shot at Dayton, who was busy reloading, but then swung round to follow her progress. His gun centred in on the fleeing woman's back as he sought a last act of malice before he was overwhelmed, but that brought him into Cassidy's full view.

Cassidy fired. His gunshot tore into

Mason's side and made him stagger forwards, but not before he'd shot at Cynthia. Cassidy saw Cynthia fall behind a table in a confusing tangle of arms and legs.

He put that sight from his mind and leapt to his feet to find that Mason had righted himself against the bar and was swinging his gun up to shoot Dayton. But before he fired, Cassidy got him in his sights.

A deadly shot to the head sent Mason spinning round to lie sprawled over the bar. He lay there until gravity dragged his body to the timbers where he twitched, then slumped, and lay flat.

Cassidy joined Dayton in hurrying across the saloon to Cynthia's side, but before he reached her, he saw the explanation for the confusing sight when she'd fallen. She hadn't been shot. At the last moment Sister Angelica had leapt out in front of her and acted as a shield.

'She saved me,' Cynthia murmured, looking up at Dayton while cradling

Sister Angelica against her chest.

'She saved us all,' Cassidy said, kneeling beside them.

'But why?'

Cassidy could only shrug, leaving Dayton to answer.

'She cared about you in that odd way of hers, but she still wanted you to choose what she thought was the right path. Perhaps she hoped that by sacrificing herself you would change your mind.'

Cynthia nodded and stroked Sister Angelica's head, her own brow furrowing with conflicting thoughts until a new voice spoke up.

'That was a good guess, but wrong.' Sister Angelica opened an eye and considered Dayton.

'And the reason?' Dayton whispered in awe when she didn't continue.

'Cynthia will work it out in her own good time.' She shrugged Cynthia's hand off her. 'And now if you'll stop fawning over me, I have work to do.'

'But you've been shot,' Cynthia

murmured, urging her with a gentle hand to stay down.

She shook her head then reached into her habit to remove the heavy cross that she wore around her neck.

'No I haven't,' she said considering the still smoking and bent metal. 'As I have always told you, this is the only protection we need.'

She tried to get to her feet, but stumbled. So on the second attempt she accepted Dayton's and Cassidy's help. She went to leave, but over by the door the habit-wearing Sherman shook his head.

'You can't go out,' he said, looking outside. 'The gunslingers were only half the problem.'

Cassidy put aside his plan to arrest Sherman on sight and joined him at the door to see what the problem was.

Outside, Redemption's townsfolk had congregated by the stables. They were armed and considering the saloon, clearly trying to work out what was happening.

'Have you annoyed them too?' Cassidy said.

'We're not popular with the townsfolk,' Sherman said. He looked at his brothers. 'But maybe it's time for that to change.'

His brothers shuffled closer and with knowing looks and raised eyebrows, a silent debate took place. Then they slipped the cowls from their heads and placed their weapons on the floor.

'This is over,' the eldest brother said.

'It is,' Sherman said. 'We made our point that men like Nelson Mann, Luther Chisholm and Mason Fox can't trample all over us. Now we will talk as equals with the railroad.'

Then, with the matter decided, side by side they trooped through the door to face the townsfolk.

15

'You want to stay?' Dayton asked, surprised that despite everything Cynthia had said and done she had chosen the one future she had claimed she didn't want.

'I do. This is a good place to be.' Cynthia considered him with a smile on her lips. 'But only if you'll come back when you can.'

'That depends on why you're staying. If it's to follow Sister Angelica into — '

The firm kiss she planted on his lips answered that question.

Then in urgent tones they talked about their plans, and to Dayton's relief, they were the ones he wanted. When he joined the others, he did so with a mixture of calmness and trepidation.

Before Cassidy took Sherman and Dayton back to Monotony, they'd returned to the Bell brothers' home to let him see the land they were protecting and show him why they'd been driven to act the way they had.

With the brothers having made their peace with the townsfolk, they had sworn an oath not to give him any trouble. Cassidy hadn't spoken since they'd made this promise, but after seeing the place where the railroad had created this situation by apparently shooting Sherman, he delivered his verdict.

'I can understand why you sought out Luther Chisholm,' he declared. 'The railroad should have talked this through and not hired gunslingers to run you off your land, but that doesn't change the fact that you killed a lawman.'

Cassidy looked at Dayton and Sherman in turn, but even though the two men hadn't had a chance to talk alone since they'd met up, Dayton had no intention of distancing himself from what had happened.

'We're both responsible,' he said. 'But it was an accident.'

'It was,' Sherman said. 'I hope I can make you believe that.'

'I hope so too,' Cassidy said after a moment's thought.

When nobody else spoke, it was left for Cynthia to ask the obvious question.

'How long will Dayton be away?'

'It's not for me to decide.' Cassidy gestured for them to join him in mounting up. 'But I reckon there'll be a railroad here when he gets back.'

Although these were the last moments he'd spend with Cynthia, Dayton couldn't bring himself to say anything to her. Instead, he cast worried glances at the greatest concern he would have while he was away: Sister Angelica.

The nun, though, took a last opportunity to glare at Cassidy.

'I expect,' she said, 'that when you return to Monotony you will waste your time in the saloon again. But you must convey to the railroad that they need to send a reasonable representative here to discuss the situation.'

'Believe me,' Cassidy said with an exasperated sigh, 'I'll tell them about you. I'm sure they'll act accordingly.'

Sister Angelica frowned, unsure whether Cassidy had paid her a compliment or an insult, but Cassidy didn't wait to hear her retort and turned his horse away.

Sherman and his brothers looked at each other, none of them feeling able to voice their thoughts. Then, after a last consideration of the gorge, Sherman mounted up.

Dayton was the last to join them. He gave Cynthia a hug, wiped away a tear that was sliding down her cheek, but when that action encouraged others to join it, he turned away. Just before he mounted his horse Sister Angelica came over.

She removed the damaged cross from her neck and looped it over his hand.

'I expect it back,' she said simply.

'I don't think it's appropriate for me,' he said, holding it out to her.

'It's appropriate for everyone. We can all do God's work in our own way. You don't have to wear a cross or be a nun to do that.'

She glanced at Cynthia then turned back with an amused smile on her lips that he knew would stop him worrying while he served his time.

He nodded then slipped the cross beneath his vest and mounted up. Then, with the twilit sky at his back, he joined the others in heading back to Monotony.

THE END

We do hope that you have enjoyed reading this large print book.

Did you know that all of our titles are available for purchase?

We publish a wide range of high quality large print books including:
Romances, Mysteries, Classics
General Fiction
Non Fiction and Westerns

Special interest titles available in large print are:
The Little Oxford Dictionary
Music Book, Song Book
Hymn Book, Service Book

Also available from us courtesy of Oxford University Press:
Young Readers' Dictionary
(large print edition)
Young Readers' Thesaurus
(large print edition)

For further information or a free brochure, please contact us at:
Ulverscroft Large Print Books Ltd.,
The Green, Bradgate Road, Anstey,
Leicester, LE7 7FU, England.
Tel: (00 44) **0116 236 4325**
Fax: (00 44) **0116 234 0205**

Other titles in the
Linford Western Library:

THE LAST GUNDOWN

Matt James

A town without mercy, a land without heart or soul: that was what bounty hunter Shell Dunbar confronted during that endless blazing summer. Even the handful of men who supported him gave him no chance of surviving that murderous summer of hate. They had already given him up for dead when he faced the last gundown . . .

DEATH RIDER

Boyd Cassidy

Mountain man Rufas Kane discovers Dan Cooper's dead body on a hillside overlooking the town of Death, leaving the townsfolk wondering why anyone would kill a harmless cowboy. Then one of Gene Adams' cowboys is killed in a gunfight with the ruthless Trey Skinner. It becomes apparent that Skinner is responsible for Cooper's death. But nothing's as it seems. That night, amid a spate of killings, Gene Adams vows to find the killer before dawn, or to die trying.

BIG TROUBLE AT FLAT ROCK

Elliot Long

Callum Bowden stared down at his adoptive father, John McKendry, lying dead in his coffin. He could barely look at the lifeless face and the silk wrapping that covered the ghastly wound across the throat . . . Meanwhile, hatred had overwhelmed Jim McKendry, who swore that someone would pay for his father's death: no matter what it took, the killer would be brought to justice — alive or dead.

RANGELAND JUSTICE

Rob Hill

Jack Just, weary from long days on the trail, rides into an isolated cattle town on the Texas panhandle. There he finds that the greedy and powerful Clovis Blacklake has the town in his pocket. But when Jack also discovers that Blacklake has cheated the town's most downtrodden inhabitant out of his rightful property, he decides to make a stand. It takes a real man to fight the ruthless Blacklake; and when Jack does, the tables begin to turn . . .